"You're Too Hard To Resist."

With a wolfish smile, Tyler reeled her in close and she knew he was going to kiss her in front of the entire bar.

And because she wanted him so badly, could feel herself rising up on to her toes to lean in to his kiss, she panicked.

Next time, hit him with this.

Susannah's words raced through her head, along with the fleeting thought that later on she'd regret this, before she reached out blindly with one hand. She had only a moment to realize that she'd grabbed the dirty spoon Tyler had been using to stuff olives with blue cheese and then she was rapping it sharply against his skull.

Tyler rubbed his head and grimaced as he smushed the blue cheese in his hair.

The crowd of onlookers had doubled in number. She threw her hands in the air. "His mother told me to do it," she announced, and marched out from behind the bar with whatever dignity remained intact.

D0725950

Dear Reader,

Welcome to another compelling month of powerful, passionate and provocative love stories from Silhouette Desire. You asked for it…you got it…more Dynasties! Our newest continuity, DYNASTIES: THE DANFORTHS, launches this month with Barbara McCauley's *The Cinderella Scandal.* Set in Savannah, Georgia, and filled with plenty of family drama and sensuality, this new twelve-book series will thrill you for the entire year.

There is one sexy air force pilot to be found between the pages of the incomparable Merline Lovelace's *Full Throttle,* part of her TO PROTECT AND DEFEND series. And the fabulous Justine Davis is back in Silhouette Desire with *Midnight Seduction,* a fiery tale in her REDSTONE, INCORPORATED series.

If it's a whirlwind Vegas wedding you're looking for (and who isn't?) then be sure to pick up the third title in Katherine Garbera's KING OF HEARTS miniseries, *Let It Ride.* The fabulous TEXAS CATTLEMAN'S CLUB: THE STOLEN BABY series continues this month with Kathie DeNosky's tale of unforgettable passion, *Remembering One Wild Night.* And finally, welcome new author Amy Jo Cousins to the Desire lineup with her superhot contribution, *At Your Service.*

I hope all of the Silhouette Desire titles this month will fulfill your every fantasy.

Melissa Jeglinski

Melissa Jeglinski
Senior Editor, Silhouette Desire

Please address questions and book requests to:
Silhouette Reader Service
U.S.: 3010 Walden Ave., P.O. Box 1325, Buffalo, NY 14269
Canadian: P.O. Box 609, Fort Erie, Ont. L2A 5X3

AT YOUR SERVICE

AMY JO COUSINS

Silhouette®

Desire

Published by Silhouette Books

America's Publisher of Contemporary Romance

If you purchased this book without a cover you should be aware
that this book is stolen property. It was reported as "unsold and
destroyed" to the publisher, and neither the author nor the
publisher has received any payment for this "stripped book."

SILHOUETTE BOOKS

ISBN 0-373-76560-6

AT YOUR SERVICE

Copyright © 2004 by Amy Jo Albinak

All rights reserved. Except for use in any review, the reproduction
or utilization of this work in whole or in part in any form by any
electronic, mechanical or other means, now known or hereafter
invented, including xerography, photocopying and recording, or in
any information storage or retrieval system, is forbidden without
the written permission of the editorial office, Silhouette Books,
233 Broadway, New York, NY 10279 U.S.A.

All characters in this book have no existence outside the imagination of
the author and have no relation whatsoever to anyone bearing the same
name or names. They are not even distantly inspired by any individual
known or unknown to the author, and all incidents are pure invention.

This edition published by arrangement with Harlequin Books S.A.

® and TM are trademarks of Harlequin Books S.A., used under license.
Trademarks indicated with ® are registered in the United States Patent
and Trademark Office, the Canadian Trade Marks Office and in other
countries.

Visit Silhouette at www.eHarlequin.com

Printed in U.S.A.

AMY JO COUSINS

loves words of all kinds, and her love of reading naturally led to a love of writing. Amy also has a passion for languages and there's nothing she likes better than learning a new language and using it to explore the history of a foreign country, whether standing on the beaches of D Day in Normandy or outside the Olympic Stadium in Munich.

Her collection of books is slowly crowding her out of her home, although her cat seems more than willing to fall asleep upon the various piles. Other than that, Amy loves learning how to do anything that takes her outdoors and away from her computer, including kayaking, sculling, rock climbing and landscape water painting.

For all the women in my life, but most of all for the number-one diva-queen-goddess, my mother.

Not many people would know that in her heart of hearts, what an eleven-year-old girl dreamed of was an electric typewriter, new or used. Thank you for always managing to give me everything I needed to pursue everything I wanted.

One

"Trust me, buddy. You want me. You need me. I know it, and you know it. Just give in to the inevitable."

Grace crossed the fingers of one hand behind her back and stuck her other hand across the bar to shake on it. The man behind the recently varnished oak counter, with the hooded, skeptical eyes and the sculpted mouth pressed closed, just stared at her. She hoped he didn't notice that her hand was shaking.

The man—Tyler, she assumed, since the banners outside read Tyler's Bar & Grill, Grand Opening Tonight—kept his unreadable, unnerving eyes on her. She was certain that a less welcoming face had never frowned on a more desperate, out-of-work woman in the world. She tugged on her newly blond hair and considered walking back out the front door before she made a complete fool of herself.

Then she remembered her original reason for walking in the bar. She'd needed change for the bus, because the only thing filling out her wallet was a single twenty-dollar bill. A job

started to sound pretty good when a girl was down to her last
twenty.

She kept her hand hanging out there over the bar and prepared to outwait this Tyler. After two weeks in hiding, she was
out of options. When she heard her grandmother's voice echo-
ing in her head, Grace wasn't surprised. She blinked back the
reflexive tears and stretched her smile a little wider.

*You're a Haley, girl, and do not forget that. You have a
genetic history of ancestors who defined the word tenacious.*

Grace knew that in all likelihood she still wouldn't have had
the nerve to face off against the ridiculously handsome man
behind the bar, except for one thing. As she'd entered the bar,
she'd had to squeeze past what looked like an entire Mexican
family, all ripping off long white aprons and shouting in gleeful
excitement. If her Spanish was good enough, she thought they
were calling out apologies to Señor Tyler because they were
leaving for Acapulco immediately, their cousin having won the
state lottery.

Tough break for this Tyler on his opening night.

She'd feel sympathetic after she talked herself into a job,
thank you very much. The muscles in her shoulder were starting to tremble from the effort of keeping her hand hanging in
midair, but she'd be damned if she'd let Mr. "I'm So Sexy"
behind the bar see that.

Not even 10:00 a.m., Tyler thought to himself, and his day
had already been flushed down the toilet. He was happy for
the Garcias—it wasn't often that good people got such a lucky
break—but having no staff did put a bit of a crimp in his Grand
Opening plans.

He'd work it out, make some phone calls, call in some fa-
vors. But all that would take time, something he was rapidly
running out of. Meanwhile, he had enough to do without dealing with the runaway teen staring determinedly across the bar
at him.

She practically had *desperate* tattooed across her forehead.
The shadows under her lake-blue eyes gave her an almost pain-

ful look of fragility. And although her hair was gloriously, deeply blond, with just enough of a hint of wave to make it slide around her cheekbones and chin and shoulders like a caress, he'd seen her tug on the ends sharply after making her ridiculous proposition. This girl was nervous enough for three ex-cons on the lam.

He felt bad about it, and took that as some consolation that he wasn't an irredeemable jerk on the sliding scale of morality, but he just didn't have time for that much trouble today. He'd been working toward this day for almost ten years, and if he wanted it to go smoothly, he didn't have time to baby-sit.

"Sorry, darlin'," he said gently, and waited to see her face fall into tears from the bold front she was putting on now. Maybe he could make it seem less personal. "You have to be over twenty-one to serve drinks in Chicago."

To his complete surprise, she laughed. Out loud and with real humor, the laughs rolling up from her belly and out past her lips in a ringing music that made him wonder what it would take to see her laugh again.

"Thank you, *darlin'*," she said, still smiling. And damned if he could stop himself from smiling back. "But if you're trying to make my day better, I'd rather have the job than the compliment."

"The compliment?" he asked.

"Tyler—you are Tyler, aren't you?" At his nod, she continued, still grinning sassily. "Well, Tyler, I could hit thirty with a short stick. So if you were trying to be tender with my feminine sensibilities, don't bother. I can't afford 'em."

It was as if she'd flipped a switch. Tyler wasn't sure what had happened, but suddenly his runaway teenager had transformed herself into the image of the smart-aleck, funny, tough woman that was his favorite kind of waitress. When she'd walked in the door of the tavern as the Garcias walked out and told him that he was going to hire her because he needed her, she was rolling on bravado alone. He'd read it in bold print across her face.

But now the confidence was real, the humor was genuine.

This blond angel was still just as easy to read, only now her face said, *I've been there, done that, and you can't even imagine what you'll be missing if you let me get away from you now.*

Still, maybe confidence that appeared so quickly would disappear just as fast. So he watched her, again, as he spoke.

"I was trying to find a nice way to tell you to get lost. I don't have a job for you."

"Nice try, buddy." She retracted the arm she'd held out over the bar, waiting for a handshake, and shook out her muscles. Her eyes pierced him like a pin through a bug on a collector's mat. "Since you're being stubborn...you just let me know when you're ready to shake on it."

She pulled out one of the narrow-backed bar stools, turned it around and stepped up to straddle it in a move that had him choking on his tongue, so suddenly did the image flow into his head of her naked and swinging a leg over him in the same arrogant way.

Get a grip, Tyler, she's looking for a job, not a bedmate, he thought. Then he watched her brace her elbows on the seatback, lace her fingers together and rest her chin on them. She licked her lips slowly, slowly enough that he could imagine what it would feel like to have her tongue gently tracing his own mouth before opening to him. The gleam in her eyes should have warned him.

"I want two bucks over minimum wage."

"What?" The outrage was genuine enough to take his mind off of her mouth. "Waitstaff get two bucks *less* than minimum, with tips to make up the difference, and you're crazy if you think you're getting any different."

"Yeah, well it looks to me like you got a problem here, Tyler. You got no staff, period. And since I'm the only one banging down your door looking for a job..."

She stared across the bar at him. He stared back. Somehow he'd gone from shooing her out the door to negotiating her hourly wage, and he hadn't even said he'd hire her yet.

Damn, she was good.

"Look, it's really a bargain, if you think about it. I'll be playing host, waiter, busboy and most likely dishwasher, too. At least at first. You're getting four employees for the price of one."

"Sounds like I'm getting four employees for two bucks over minimum. That's a lot higher than one measly server."

"Like I said, darlin'—" She shook back her hair and sat up straight. "You need me. You want me. You know it and I know it."

The trouble was, she was right. He did need her, and he did want her. And if he needed and wanted for two different reasons, then that was his problem. The boss sleeping with the help was the fastest way to lose good workers. And he'd already learned how quickly a woman tired of a man who spent more time with his business than he did with her. He wouldn't be walking down that road again.

He listened to his own thoughts and gave up the battle. He'd already decided to hire her, assuming her references panned out. He didn't really have much of a choice.

"Just give in to the inevitable, hmm?"

"You got it," she said, and winked at him. And Tyler was sold. She was perfect.

"Where have you worked before here?"

The question was a casual one, meant more to be social than as a background check. Anyone who'd waited tables for a month or two would be able to handle his straightforward menu and small seating area. So he was a little curious when she paused before answering him.

"At a diner." He watched her tug nervously on her hair again before shrugging at him from across the bar. "We were open twenty-four-seven. Heavy late-night and breakfast crowds. But you could do your nails and the *New York Times*'s crossword between noon and midnight."

Something indefinable, something suddenly not quite right, kept him asking questions.

"What was the name of the place?"

Again the hesitation. And when she answered him, he knew he had her.

"Mel's Diner."

Grace saw Tyler's eyes widen, in disbelief, she assumed, and cursed herself for a fool. She should never have walked in here without laying out her story beforehand. When he'd asked her that stupid question, her mind had blanked and she'd blurted out the first thing that had popped into her head.

If she didn't think fast, she'd lose this job before she had a chance to tie on an apron.

"Mel's Diner? Oh, darlin', that's rich." For the first time since she walked in the door, he turned his back on her and went back to stocking glasses on the shelves behind the bar. "You had me believing you, too. But watching a bunch of wise-talking, butt-shaking waitresses on a 70's TV sitcom does not make you one. Nice try, sweets, but no cigar."

Grace rolled her eyes in frustration and tried to think fast, something that was definitely easier without his eyes on her. Did the man have to be gorgeous enough to make it difficult for her to think straight? She knew that in her old life she would have handled someone like Tyler without flinching, secure in her job, her family, her position in the world.

But now she had no job and no family to help her define herself. And she couldn't very well tell the man that up until two weeks ago she'd been in charge of eleven of the top-grossing restaurants in Chicago. She was stuck with lying, and knowing she wasn't very good at it made her nervous. Looking at Tyler made her even more nervous.

Get a grip, girl, she told herself. You have no backup here, no money and no choice. She'd managed to talk herself most of the way into a job by imagining what her grandmother would have said if she were stuck in this bizarre situation and pretending to be her. So she'd just keep doing that until she convinced this Tyler to hire her.

"You think that's funny, huh?" She made her voice sound loud and confident and just a little bit annoyed. "It's not so amusing when the guy who hires you hands you a pink dress and a frilly white apron as a uniform and tells you that you get a bonus if you say 'Kiss my grits!' once an hour.''

After a moment Tyler turned slowly back around to face her and she saw him fight to keep the smile under wraps. She'd really put her heart into the imitation of the TV waitress, Alice, and knew the voice sounded funny coming out of her mouth.

''Did you chew gum?''

She drew a cross over her heart with one finger. ''It was part of my job description.'' She paused. ''My manager had a cardboard cutout of Alice standing by the front door. He kissed it every night when he left. I couldn't make this up if I tried.''

And then he did laugh, and she knew she was safe. She'd pulled it off. The relief was strong enough to make her glad she was sitting down.

''What's your name?''

''Grace,'' she said. The feeling of having escaped from danger was overwhelming, but she still remembered to use her mother's maiden name. ''Grace Desmond.''

The danger returned with Tyler's next words.

''Okay, Grace Desmond. Consider yourself hired. Grand Opening is at 5:00 p.m. tonight, so show up back here at three and we'll fill out your paperwork. Bring your license and some other kind of ID, and an apron if you have one. If not, I'll give you one.''

Grace was shaking her head yes, in agreement, even as her mind started to panic. There was no way she could show this man her driver's license. Even if he didn't recognize her family name as one of the most prominent in Chicago, the address on her identification was not one a diner waitress could possibly have. Not unless she had a wealthy benefactor.

Tyler stretched a hand across the bar, ready to shake on it at last. For a moment Grace just stared at his hand, wide-palmed and strong, showing scars around the knuckles that spoke of hard work and harder play. Then she reached out and fit her own, smaller hand into his and shook on her new job.

When she tried to pull her hand away, he didn't let go. She

glanced up sharply at him, concerned. His dark eyes seemed to swallow all the light in the room as he leaned forward, gaze locked on her face, and pressed a kiss to her knuckles. She could feel the shape of his mouth on her fingers, the dampness of the inner edge of his lips catching on her skin. All over her body, muscles froze tightly in place to keep from shivering as Tyler slowly dragged his lips from side to side just once.

"And I'll need a reference. Before you leave."

She waited until she turned the corner and was sure he couldn't see her from the bar windows before breaking into a run. She'd gone at least two blocks without seeing a pay phone anywhere when she remembered the cellular phone in her purse.

Surely they couldn't be tracing her cell phone. Wasn't that impossible? Grace decided to keep the conversation short.

She dug the phone out, flipped it open and dialed the number from heart. While she listened to the electronic rings chirping in her ear and prayed that Paul would be home, she remembered the look in Tyler's eyes as he'd folded up the napkin on which she'd written the name and telephone number of her reference. She didn't know if he was trying to intimidate her into the truth or to seduce her, but she was afraid that he might do both.

"Hello?" a grumpy, hoarse voice finally answered.

"Paul? Thank God, you're home."

"Where the damn else would I be at this ridiculous hour of the morning? And who is this calling me?"

"It's going on eleven in the morning, Paul. Are you sure Louis can handle the lunch crowd at Nîce without you?" she teased. The little stab of pain at the thought of her favorite restaurant was ignored.

"Gracie?" She could hear him coming out of sleep, her mentor, her good friend, and today, hopefully, her savior. "Is this my little Gracie?

"*Bien sûr, Paul,*" she reassured him in his native French. "Have you missed me?"

"Missed you? You little brat, I am crazy with worry about you. I can't cook. Where are you? Are you well?"

Grace felt her breath catch and the tears start to collect at the corner of her eyes. For the first time in weeks she was talking to someone who really cared about her, and the warmth in Paul's voice was nearly enough to break her. As she took a deep breath, trying for control, she realized that Paul was still speaking to her.

"—*absolument* crazy around here without you. Your family talk of hiring an investigator. And your fiancé, that *crétin*, trying to take over my restaurant. Listen, *chérie*, tell me where you are and I send a taxi to get you and bring you here. And then we straighten this whole mess out."

Investigator.

That one word was enough to snap her back to reality, which was that she was standing on a street corner in full view of the world, talking on her cell phone, and meanwhile her family, not to mention Charles, might have already hired someone to try to track her down. To bring her back.

"Paul," she broke into his stream of words. "Paul, listen to me. First of all, Charles and I are *not* engaged, no matter what the family says. I never said yes. And I'll discuss everything else with you later, but right now I need you to do me a favor. Please."

"You know you have only to ask," he answered immediately, the solid strength of his voice reassurance in itself.

"This is going to sound crazy, Paul, but I need you to be a reference for me so I can get a job waiting tables." She repeated the description of the diner that she'd given to Tyler, although since Paul wasn't familiar with the 70's sitcom she'd based her story on, there was some confusion as to why he would ever let one of his employees chew gum. Not to mention the famous quote.

"I have eaten these grits, yes? And that was bad enough. But why would anyone want to kiss them, *chérie?*"

By the time she explained to Paul what he would need to say, and described what might show up on his caller ID to alert him to answer the phone "Mel's Diner," she was frantic to get off the phone.

"Thank you, Paul. You are saving my life."

"I still don't understand why you want to wait tables when you should be running *all* of your family's restaurants. You know that's what your grandmother wanted. But if it will help you, and if you promise to call me soon…"

"I will, Paul. I promise."

After a sweaty walk during which she seriously mourned not having her personal driver still available to her, Grace made it back to the kitchenette room she was renting at the Sherradin Hotel. She watched the cockroaches scatter as she opened the door and let in the light from the hall. The bright September sunshine outside couldn't penetrate the grime covering the small windows.

"Olly, olly, oxen-free," she murmured, reminded of games she'd played as a child where everyone scattered into hiding places and waited for whoever was It to come and find them. She wondered how long it would take her to make enough money for a deposit on a better room.

And how are you going to rent an apartment, Ms. Grace *Desmond,* without any identification to show a landlord? she asked herself. Not to mention convince Tyler to keep you on.

"I don't know," she answered out loud, "but I have to get out of this pathetic excuse for a hotel. I don't care how they spell it. I am never going to think I'm staying at a Sheraton."

The single room had a bright overhead light and a sturdy lock on the door, and that was about all that could be said about it of a positive nature. On this hot, late summer day, the air was positively stifling since air-conditioning was a luxury definitely not found here. Never in her life had she lived without climate control. The discomfort of it was a revelation she'd not been thrilled to have.

Grace had bought a cheap set of blue-striped sheets and some brightly colored plastic glasses and plates, so she knew those were clean. But rusty water stains spread menacingly on the ceiling above her bed and the short pile of the beige carpet showed a dozen stains of its own. She didn't know what had made those irremovable marks, but she was unfortunately sure that, unlike the ceiling, they weren't water.

She yanked open the folding door of the one skinny closet and then cursed as the door came off its track again. Her battle with the closet door had become a daily ritual, one that Grace never seemed to win. She tugged various items off their hangers and laid them out on her bed, planning for the evening ahead of her.

She knew from experience that opening night of a new restaurant was insanity personified in a space bounded by four walls, a ceiling and a floor. And that was true even if the staff was well-trained and comfortable with the menu and ordering system. Grace knew she would pick up Tyler's system quickly. In fact, she'd be surprised if he had much of a system at all set up yet.

But she hadn't stuck around to ask him if he would be able to find fill-in staff for tonight's shift, and if so, how many people he might be able to dig up.

Worst case scenario, she imagined, would have her greeting people at the door, seating them, taking orders, serving drinks and food, clearing tables and washing dishes in the kitchen. As long as he didn't expect her to cook, they might actually stumble their way through the evening intact.

Just in case, though, she selected clothes that looked quietly chic, yet were sturdy enough to stand being splashed by or soaked in various liquids and solids. Black, straight-cut pants that wouldn't show spills. A white blouse made from a fabric absolutely not found in nature, but that miraculously refused to stain—even red wine rinsed out of it with a splash of club soda. The shoes she dragged out from the bottom of the closet were black lace-ups that looked contemporary, with a short stacked heel, and had the most expensive arch support inserts on the market hidden in them.

She hadn't thought to bring any aprons with her from the restaurant on the day she'd fled her family and their demands.

She hadn't thought much at all that day, Grace admitted to herself. She'd simply left work, packed a bag at her condo and decided to disappear.

And disappear she had, for the past two weeks, using the time to sit in diners and coffee bars and trying to think of a solution to her problems. But now she was running out of cash, and she knew that withdrawing money from her bank account or using checks or credit cards would leave an easily followed trail.

She'd thought it would be easy enough for her to get a job, at least a low-paying one. And here Grace laughed at herself. She'd conveniently blinded herself to the reality of life, which was that without ID or personal references, the average person on the street wasn't going to trust her with a dime, much less a job or an apartment.

Tyler certainly isn't likely to allow me to stick around for long as a mystery lady, she thought.

The stress of the day swept over her in a slowly crashing wave and she felt herself on the edge of tears for the second time that day.

I need a nap. Just an hour nap, and then I can figure out a way to make him keep me on. He wouldn't be the first restaurant owner to pay staff under the table.

She stretched out across the top sheet on her bed and snagged her travel alarm clock off of the nightstand. Just an hour, she thought hazily, and then I'll figure it all out. She pressed the buttons and flipped the switch that would wake her up at one o'clock in the afternoon.

Her eyes were already closed as she fumbled the alarm back onto the nightstand. And as her brain slowly shut down, she was left with a single image floating in the last, dreamy layers of thought. The image of Tyler, the widening pools of his dark, almost-midnight eyes staring at her over her own hand as he moved his lips over her skin.

She dreamed, as she drifted off, and in her dreams Tyler's mouth slid from her hand to glide up her arm. His lips grazed across her shoulder and trailed slowly up to her mouth, leaving starflower kisses glowing faintly against her skin as she dreamed of them in the night. And when he left her, in her dream, the skin of her body was flushed and glowing with the light of the stars, absolutely everywhere.

Three hours later, when she pushed open the restaurant door and stepped inside to coolness, only to stop short at the sight of Tyler, she knew she was in trouble. The incredibly sensual dreams of her afternoon nap were one thing—and a pleasure she figured she was allowed to indulge in, since it was only a dream. But here she was, damn near drooling at the sight of him, and the man had his back to her while he spoke on the phone, for crying out loud.

"You're staring at the back of his head, Grace. No big deal," she muttered to herself.

But there was something in the way he ran his fingers through his hair that made her want to take over the job herself. Run her own fingers through the thick, dark hair that was overly due for a cut, and smooth it back to order for him.

"Thanks a million, angel. You're redeeming my faith in women. See you in an hour."

She heard him chuckle and say goodbye to the woman on the other end of the phone line, and repressed the urge to find out who the woman was and to scratch her eyes out. Sheesh, her hormones must be on overdrive.

Think bossman, not boyfriend, she repeated to herself silently.

"Your reference checked out fine. Great, even. Although you should tell that guy to cut out the fake French accent."

She didn't think he'd noticed her come in. His back to the door still, redialing the phone, Tyler reached behind him and placed some papers and a pen on the bar.

"Just fill these out, you can skip the references part, and we'll get you set up."

For five minutes he chatted up what sounded like yet another woman on the phone, his voice coaxing seductively, promising anything. Meanwhile, Grace filled out her fake name, and hotel address, and then stared blankly at the lines requesting her driver's license and social security numbers. She hadn't figured out a way to wriggle out of this part yet.

When Tyler hung up the phone and finally turned toward her, she flinched involuntarily and started digging through her purse, looking for inspiration.

"Not done yet?" he asked, looking at the half-completed form.

"Um, no," she mumbled as she shoved her wallet to the bottom of her purse. Then she put on her most innocent, worried look and tilted the purse so that he could look in to see the tangle of makeup and scrap paper. "I think I left my wallet back in my room."

With any luck, her new boss would just think she was a little flighty, and not a little con artist.

Her luck held.

"Bring it tomorrow," he said shortly. Punching a button on the register, he popped the cash drawer open and tugged out two twenties. He handed them across the bar to Grace. "Somehow, we didn't get any limes or lemons with our produce delivery this morning. Not a good thing for a bar. I want you to get as many of each as you can."

The request was made as casually as if she'd worked for him for years, but Grace still felt as though she was being tested. She wondered what odds he was putting on her returning with the fruit and banished her irritation at being under suspicion. Hopefully, the idea that she'd run off with his cash was the long shot in his mind.

"I don't really know the neighborhood. I'm sorry."

"For what?"

She'd apologized automatically, somehow feeling the need to atone for the theft she knew he imagined.

"There's a store two blocks north on Linden," he continued. "Make it fast. We've got a lot of work to do still."

She slid off the stool and flew out the front door of the bar. Feeling as though she'd just received a Get-Out-of-Jail-Free card in a Monopoly game, she was halfway to the store before she realized that she hadn't really escaped anything. She would still have to figure out how she could get around showing him an ID.

Tyler might not worry about filling out her paperwork for a day or two, but Grace knew that wouldn't last. Sooner or later he'd remember that he had yet to see any form of identification from her. She would count on making herself invaluable to the man before that point.

Even if she only had tonight, she'd do it. She'd make Tyler think he couldn't live without her.

Strange lady, Tyler thought as he continued making the necessary calls to come up with at least a skeleton staff for the night. She'd practically begged him for this job, but she'd rushed out the door on his errand as though she'd just been let out of prison.

The ever-present nervousness in her vivid blue eyes contrasted sharply with the delicate grace of her features. She looked as if she constantly expected him to snap at her. And she had definitely been aware of his spontaneous honesty test. He'd seen the flare of anger she quickly suppressed when she realized he thought she might take his money and run.

He was actually fairly certain she'd return, produce in hand, if for no other reason than to prove his suspicions wrong. What disturbed him was the feeling that he'd be far more than a little disappointed if she didn't come back. Tyler told himself that it was just that he needed her for the job, but knew that his concern ran deeper than that, even after only a few hours.

Shrugging off his uneasy thoughts, he dialed the next number and waited for the female voice that eventually answered.

"Hi, sweetheart. Tell me you're not doing anything exciting tonight. I need you badly."

Two

Right up until the moment when the three-year-old at table six nailed her on the chin with a maraschino cherry, Grace thought the night was going fairly well.

Even as the little demon's parents apologized frantically for his assault with a flying garnish, Grace just shook her head and marched straight to the rear of the restaurant. She pushed the swinging doors to the kitchen hard enough to set them flapping on their hinges and threw her tray on a stainless-steel counter.

"I quit," she announced to the room in general. "It is a complete madhouse out there and I'd rather shovel manure for a living than bring another Shirley Temple to that little monster at table six."

The faces that turned toward her from the grill and the dishwasher were female and smiling widely at her threat.

It was the fourth time she'd quit since the doors had opened at 5:00 p.m. She supposed her threats didn't carry much weight anymore.

"C'mon, Grace," Sarah called cheerfully from where she

stood at the sink, up to her elbows in soapy water and dirty plates. "You're the only one of us who knows what she's doing. You were certainly right that I'd help out most by scrubbing pots."

Grace flushed with guilt as she remembered how she'd banished Sarah to the kitchen to wash dishes after the second time Sarah had dropped a trayful of drinks in one hour. The man Sarah had drenched with Merlot and beer had only settled down after she'd comp'ed his meal.

"I shouldn't have told you what to do, Sarah. After all, you're doing Tyler a favor just by helping out."

"Don't be ridiculous. I'm clearly not cut out for waiting tables, and if somebody didn't wash these dishes, we'd run out of plates to serve dinner on fast enough." Sarah grinned at her and blew sweaty bangs off her forehead with a puff of breath. The ponytail she'd pulled her hair into was wilting rapidly in the steamy heat of the dish room.

"Besides, if a sister won't scrub pots for her brother, then who will?" Sarah asked and shook her butt to the music spilling out of the boom box on the dishrack behind her.

Sarah's easy acquiescence to Grace's taking charge was only the latest in a string of surprises.

Grace's first surprise had come when she'd returned to the restaurant, after getting just a tiny bit lost on her errand, to find the tables set, the soup of the day simmering and the makings of a restaurant staff ready to pitch in for the evening. By the time she'd been introduced to Addy, Sarah and Max, Tyler's older and two younger sisters, respectively, and Susannah, his mother, Grace was spinning in a whirlwind of names and unfairly beautiful dark-haired women.

"Mom, bless her beautiful heart, is going to cook." A snort of laughter from his mother made them all laugh. "You'll be fine, Mom. The Garcias did most of the prep work before they left. It's just like cooking dinner for six, only I hope you'll have to do that twenty or thirty times. Max, you've got a year to go before you're old enough to serve drinks, so you probably ought to help out in the kitchen. Sarah and Addy, one of you helps Grace wait tables, the other can bus them and set 'em up. Gracie's done this all a million times, so she'll tell you what to do.''

And with that, he'd walked away to answer the phone, leaving her with a stack of aprons and order pads and four women looking to her for direction.

"Great, Tyler. That's just great,'' she muttered, and thought furiously about what to do next. She'd seen at once as Tyler passed out assignments that Sarah was terrified about waiting tables and that Max was annoyed to be stuck in the kitchen with her mother.

But I'm not in charge here, and according to what I've told Tyler, all I've ever done is wait tables in a diner. I don't want to look too comfortable with authority here, if I'm going to convince everyone that I'm just another waitress.

Her first question was for Susannah, Tyler's mother.

"Do you think you'll be able to make everything on the menu? If you have any problems, we can always say that we didn't receive a delivery of something crucial and apologize for the dish not being available.''

The older woman raised one eyebrow archly and smiled. "Tyler came to me for help in designing the menu, because he likes my cooking. If I have problems with anything on that list, he'll laugh me out of kitchen.'' She turned and walked off to the kitchen.

"Terrific. Two minutes and I've already pissed off the boss's mom.'' She kept her voice low enough that she hoped no one heard her. Then she caught Sarah grinning at her.

"Okay, everyone grab an order pad. We're going to make cheat sheets, so you don't have to keep looking at the menu for prices. You, too, Max, just in case,'' she said, trying to include the girl who had her arms crossed over her chest and a shuttered stare.

She kitted them all out with a three-pocket apron, order book and pad, and a tray for serving drinks. When she wrapped the apron strings twice around her waist, tied them in front of her and stuffed her book in the center apron pocket, she was surprised at how at home she felt. It had been years since she'd worked as a server at a restaurant, but apparently waiting tables was like riding a bike.

Once you did it, you never forgot how.

"Okay, ladies. Lesson number one. The customer is always right." Grace waited a beat. "Except when they are obnoxious, crazy or just plain wrong."

They laughed and then listened as Grace gave them a crash course in how to wait tables. From greeting the customers and taking orders, to serving food and cashing out a check. When the three sisters were temporarily occupied with an argument over the most efficient way to abbreviate garnishes and side orders, Grace took a moment to search out Tyler.

She found him in a tiny office, hidden behind a door off the kitchen. When she turned the knob, the door opened and she carefully peeked her head into the room.

Tyler sat at a desk overflowing with paperwork. Grace saw stacks of invoices teetering precariously on one edge and a hastily assembled pile of applications at Tyler's other elbow. The man himself was on the phone and as she listened to the conversation, she understood that he was trying to find more permanent help than his sisters and mother for the restaurant.

"No, thanks, Jorge. I'm covered for the weekend. But if you could start on Monday, you'd be a lifesaver, man."

He noticed her waiting and waved her into the office with a flick of his hand. She leaned against the doorjamb and crossed her arms to wait. He was off the phone in short order, after thanks and goodbyes.

"How are things on the floor with my crazy sisters?"

"Everything's in order, bossman." She snapped him a two-finger salute that was lacking enough in respect to have her doing two hundred push-ups if she'd been at boot camp. But she couldn't hide her fondness for the women arguing loudly in the front of the house as she kept speaking, her voice forceful. "And your sisters aren't crazy. They're wonderful. You should be proud to have them for family."

"I am."

His simple answer stopped her and made her flush. She couldn't keep on overreacting and being this easily flustered around him. She'd managed herself well enough around the rest of his family. Well, except for his mother.

The fact that she was basically comfortable around everyone except the only man in the restaurant did not escape her.

I'll get over it, Grace told herself.

I'll have to.

"Sorry." Her apology was awkward. "I just came in to ask if you had a price list for drinks."

"Of course." Tyler stood and reached out to a shelf above her head, abutting the door frame. He deliberately crowded her as he searched for the price list in the stack of papers piled haphazardly on the shelf. He waited for her to back up, and smiled to himself when she just glared up at him, those lake-blue eyes flashing with waves of irritation.

He'd left his door open a crack after walking off and leaving Grace to whip his sisters into shape as a waitstaff. He heard her unintentionally insult his mother and flinched in sympathy. And then, after a moment of silence during which he could somehow *feel* her take a deep breath and take charge, he heard his fragile, blond smart-ass launch into an entertaining and informative lecture on how to wait tables like a pro. After five minutes, he'd shut his office door and tackled the phone.

Now he listened to her making huffy little noises of irritation as he pretended to continue his search for a price list and he wanted to laugh out loud at what a bundle of nerves and brashness she was. Making a noise of sudden, pleased discovery, he exaggerated his relief at finding the laminated sheet of paper and sat again, handing it to her in the process.

"Thanks." She started to glance over the list as she turned to go, then stopped short in the doorway.

"This isn't going to work."

"What isn't going to work?" he asked, his voice sharper than he'd intended. He'd put a lot of thought into the pricing of his drinks, after all, searching for that delicate balance between maximizing profit and convincing the customer that he was getting a good deal. Ten years of serving drinks in someone else's bar had taught him what worked and he knew his price list was exactly right for the house.

He saw Grace turn and glance guiltily at him, and wondered what misdeed she thought she'd performed now. When she brushed off his question with a shrug and an apology, he realized that she was afraid to point out to him something she didn't agree with. He gentled his voice. Another of his goals was to be the kind of boss that employees felt comfortable talking to.

"It's okay, Grace. I'm not going to be mad at you. If you've got a suggestion, let me have it. It's our opening night, you know. I probably don't have everything perfect yet." He smiled to encourage her.

Grace fumed and kept the timid smile plastered across her face. Not until Tyler had snapped at her had she realized that she'd slipped and started talking to him as a restaurant manager would. That level of confidence and analysis would certainly be out of character for her cover story.

"No, you do. Have things perfect, I mean. The prices seem right-on for the neighborhood and the crowd you're likely to get." She kept her voice soft and on the nervous side. "I was just thinking that this list might be a little complicated for your sisters. Seeing as it's their first time waiting tables."

"And what would you suggest?"

"Well, if we could maybe group the drinks into just a few price categories? You know, domestic and import beers, well drinks, call drinks and premiums." She reeled off the standard ordering procedure of her restaurants without a hitch. "That way they wouldn't have so much to remember."

Tyler knew immediately that she was correct and was irritated for not thinking of it himself. He might have the time and inclination to memorize fifty or sixty different drink prices, but his servers deserved a price list they could learn without studying as if they were prepping for a college exam. After a moment's thought, he grabbed a piece of scrap paper and scribbled out a new list that was five lines long.

"For tonight, use this. We'll expand it later."

"Thank you, Tyler. This will help out a lot."

It was like a punch to the gut, grabbing him and dragging him to his feet to stand over her. Just hearing her say his name in that soft, almost-apologetic voice, as though she was afraid even to speak to him. It made him want to kiss her until she pushed him away—he had no doubt that she would—and told him off again in that sassy, take-no-grief attitude.

He snagged her elbow as she headed out the door and pulled her back around to face him. Her eyes were wide and blinking with nervousness as he laid a hand alongside her face and brushed his fingers from her hairline to the edge of her mouth.

"In the future, don't hesitate to talk to me, Grace."

He leaned forward, close enough to feel the warmth of her breath on his face.

"You don't have to hide your intelligence from me. Let me into that clever little mind."

His lips hovered over hers for one never-ending moment.

"I want to know what you're thinking."

When he touched his mouth to hers, she gave a little sigh and sank the smallest bit further into his kiss. Her mouth eased open under his gentle assault, his teeth nipping softly at her full, lower lip. He traced his fingertips along the edge of her upswept hair, around to the back of her neck and then skated them down her spine. Her back arched sharply beneath his hand. She might have been avoiding the pressure of his hand, but her escape had the pleasant side effect of pressing her breasts into his chest.

Tyler felt light-headed from the effort of restraining himself from moving any faster and scaring her off. Well, if he passed out, surely someone would throw some water on him to wake him up.

When she pulled back after a time that was not nearly long enough, Tyler figured that that was to be expected.

Her next words, however, were not.

"I'm thinking Addy and Sarah aren't going to be able to handle more than two tables each, which leaves me with eight four-tops and hostess duties."

"What?"

"You asked me what I was thinking." She looked up at him with calm eyes. "That's it."

For a moment Tyler was offended. He'd kissed her and she'd practically knocked him out, and she felt nothing? She could just continue a conversation as if nothing had happened between them? Fine, then. If she could ignore it, so could he.

But as he opened his mouth to say something that would probably have turned out to be irredeemably callous, he saw Grace raise her hand.

She dropped it down again by her side a second later, but he'd caught the nervous gesture. She'd been reaching to tug on her hair, but couldn't because she'd pinned her hair up in a loose twist. Taking a second look, he noticed the faint flush on her cheekbones that hadn't been there before and the barely visible flutter of an elevated pulse at the base of her throat. She'd been as affected by the brief kiss as he was, he realized.

Tyler knew the satisfaction he felt at these signs was a ridiculous display of his male ego, but what the hell. He could afford to indulge himself. He'd made Grace blush.

The smile he shot her was pure lord-of-the-manor.

"Sounds like you've got it covered then, darlin'. Good thing, 'cause we open the door in fifteen minutes, and soon after, all hell breaks loose. I hope."

Grace nodded, muttered something incoherent and walked off through the kitchen, heading back to the floor of the house. And Tyler sat in his swivel chair, kicked his feet up on the desk and started counting all the reasons that it was a bad idea for him to be feeling this attracted to his waitress, the only non-family staff member he had at the moment.

But he grinned as he counted.

As Grace fled through the kitchen, she kept her head down. The sound of a pot banging loudly on a steel counter made her flinch and then groan out loud. Oh, Lord. She hadn't even thought about Tyler's mother being right outside his office, prepping food for the night.

She wondered if there was any possible recovery from insulting the woman and then kissing her son, who was supposed to be her boss, in front of her.

Maybe she would just tell all her customers that there would be no food served tonight and stay out of the kitchen completely. Hey, they could still drink.

Just not eat.

But damn the man, did he have to just go and kiss her?

She was already having trouble enough, concentrating around him, trying not to trip over her own tongue or her false stories. She just couldn't seem to catch her balance when she was in the same room as Tyler, and she wasn't quite sure why.

Okay, sure, the man was movie-star handsome. The kind of movie star that was inevitably referred to as having "rugged, good looks." Which in Tyler's case meant a heavy, sensuous mouth, cheekbones to die for and straight, dark brows over midnight eyes. Eyes whose favorite activity seemed to be taking long, sweeping looks over her body with half-lidded lazy indulgence. And it wasn't fair that although she was tall enough at five foot nine to look most men in the eyes, she had to crane her neck to look up at Tyler when she spoke to him. But after all, the man was just a bartender.

A gorgeous, hardworking, restaurant-opening bartender, whose family obviously adored him.

But still, Grace argued with herself. She'd arranged cocktail parties for industry magnates, hosted political fund-raisers for senators and congresswomen and arranged for film and music celebrities to dine in her restaurants in privacy.

The vice president of the United States had given a speech at one of her restaurants during the Democratic National Convention, for crying out loud.

In all those different situations, Grace had kept her cool. She'd refrained from acting star-struck by actors who, when she was a girl, had shaped her idea of what handsome was, or intimidated by the men and women she met who had the power to alter the course of her country's destiny.

But Tyler didn't even have to touch her to make her lose her train of thought.

And when he did touch her…

Be honest, Grace, you lost your mind. Completely.

She decided that a bathroom visit was in order, if only to make sure that she didn't look as disheveled as she felt. She hadn't been in the ladies' room yet, but it was easy enough to find. She'd just straighten herself up a bit. Perhaps reapply a little of the lipstick Tyler had kissed off her mouth.

Ten seconds later she was back in the dining room, grabbing a protesting Addy and Sarah by the hands and dragging them into the bathroom.

She flung open the door and waved *ta-da* with one hand.

"Have you *seen* this bathroom?"

Sarah and Addy looked at each other and then back at Grace, before Sarah said cautiously, "Yes. Why? Don't you like it?"

"Like it?" Grace stared dreamily at the charming little room in front of her. The walls were painted in blue-on-blue sponge paint and were hung with dried floral wreaths. Instead of a harsh overhead light, small shaded lamps were scattered around the room. A basket of potpourri, along with other baskets containing complimentary sample-size toiletries, sat alongside the marble sink. Even the floor was unique with a jigsaw puzzle pattern of flagstones in several muted colors. "I'd come to eat here just for the pleasure of visiting the ladies' room."

"I know what you mean," Addy murmured as the three women stood in the doorway and experienced a moment of pure, feminine pleasure.

"Which one of you is responsible for this? Or was it your mother?"

"Neither," answered Sarah with a smug grin on her face.

"Then who—not Tyler?"

"None other," Addy chipped in helpfully while pulling back her masses of wildly curly hair and attempting to impose some kind of order on the tangles. "He said that after a lifetime of listening to us complain about how awful women's bathrooms usually were, he wanted to make sure we'd have nothing bad to say about his.''

Just what I need, Grace thought. Gorgeous, hardworking *and* he listens to his sisters.

She didn't realize that she'd spoken out loud until both Sarah and Addy erupted with laughter.

''Sounds like Grace has the hots for our brother dearest, doesn't it, Addy?''

''Sure does. We'll have to check her out, you know. Make sure she's good enough for him,'' Addy teased. ''Spill it, Gracie. Where'd you grow up? Go to school? Does insanity generally run in your family?''

''Good question, sis,'' Sarah quipped back. ''Because you knew she's got to be a little bit crazy to go for our brother. Even if he is gorgeous.''

''But pushy. Don't forget that. He can be a real pain in the—''

''Listen.'' The word came out sharper than she intended. ''I don't have the hots for Tyler.'' She regretted the words already as she watched herself kill the laughter in the air. She knew they were joking about checking out her background, but she couldn't stop the fear that rushed through her at the words. And she couldn't begin to answer their teasing questions without making up even more lies. ''I don't have the hots for anyone, and I certainly wouldn't be dumb enough to get involved with my boss, in any case. That would be completely inappropriate.''

Sarah's face froze, then drained of color. She crossed her hands over her chest and rubbed her arms tightly. Grace wondered if she'd just delivered yet another unintentional but deadly insult and hoped she was wrong.

''I'm sorry.'' Grace looked Sarah in the eyes as she spoke. ''But maybe we should get ready. We'll be opening the doors in a minute.''

''Sure,'' the other woman said and walked away.

Grace turned to Addy, wanting to apologize further, and saw

that the older woman was watching her sister leave and looking concerned. As if she felt the weight of Grace's gaze, Addy shrugged and lifted her hands in a helpless gesture.

"I was afraid she was dating that jerk of a boss she has. You just confirmed it for me."

"Addy, I'm sorry." It felt as though she was doing nothing but saying she was sorry to these women, who were being so nice to her, for what must look like hypersensitivity and a brusqueness that bordered on rudeness. "I didn't mean to make Sarah feel bad. I wasn't even thinking about her." She shook her head in frustration. Maybe she would be better off if these women didn't like her. She really shouldn't get involved here.

Somehow, that didn't seem possible though. And she did feel bad. "I didn't even know she *had* a boss."

Addy reached out with a strong and graceful hand and squeezed Grace's shoulder in sympathy.

"Don't worry about it, sweetie. You couldn't have known, and we're all a little nervous tonight." She smiled gently. "What do you say we get ready for the ravenous hordes?"

Grace decided that there was one last thing she needed to do first.

Palms sweating like a teenager's in the principal's office, she marched straight back to the kitchen and, after a brief hesitation, slipped quietly through the swinging doors.

Tyler's mother was separated from her by the prep counter, over which she'd hand the dishes to the servers, and a stainless steel-top island that served both as chopping block and counter space. As Grace watched, Susannah wielded a large knife on a head of broccoli, slicing up florets as though the tough, fibrous stalks were made of butter.

Don't slouch, girl. She could hear her grandmother's voice admonishing her. *What do you think she's going to do? Bite you?*

You never know, Grace retorted, and then gave in.

"Mrs., um," she began, and then realized that she had no idea what Susannah's surname was. "Susannah? Excuse me?"

"Yes? And it's Mrs. Tyler, but that makes me feel old, so don't call me that." Susannah looked up from her chopping.

"Okay," Grace said, confused. "Then Tyler is his last name?"

"Yes."

"What's his first name?"

Susannah scowled. "That boy. I gave him a perfectly good name and he won't let anyone use it. His name is Christopher."

"I don't understand. Christopher is a very ordinary—" she saw the frown deepen "—I mean, a very lovely name. Why doesn't he like it?"

Tyler's mother blushed faintly. "Because of his middle name. I keep telling him I was delirious, after eighteen hours of labor with his fat head. His father and I had already decided on Christopher for a first name, but we hadn't picked a middle name yet."

"So what did you decide on?"

"Robin." Grace choked on a giggle. Susannah grimaced. "I told you I was delirious. I thought it was charming."

"Christopher Robin?"

"As in Winnie the Pooh, yes. You see why he hates me. He's refused to answer to anything but Tyler ever since first grade."

Grace couldn't think of anything to say. Moments ticked by in silence until she remembered her original reason for coming into the kitchen. She noticed that Susannah hadn't put the knife down. No time like the present, she thought.

"I just wanted to apologize if I offended you earlier. I assure you I meant no disrespect when I questioned your cooking abilities." She was proud to hear that her voice sounded steady and sincere. Since she hadn't been thrown out of the kitchen yet, she thought it time to try a little charm. "My mother only goes in the kitchen to use the phone to order take-out. I've learned not to make any assumptions about mothers and cooking. But I'm glad you'll be in charge here."

"In charge?" Susannah laughed and the smile carved well-worn tracks in her still lovely face. "You don't know my son very well if you think anyone but himself is in charge at this restaurant. This is his baby.''

"I don't know your son at all, ma'am,'' Grace said, letting her frustration show. She caught herself reaching to tug on her hair again and tried to force herself to stay still. But the frustration was pushing at her self-control and she couldn't quite hide the irritation in her voice. "I don't know him. I don't have the hots for him. And I certainly don't want to get involved with him!''

She punctuated each sentence with a pointed finger at Tyler's mother and before she even finished the last words was already horrified by her outburst.

"So was that someone else I saw kissing him in the office doorway?''

"Oh, God, I was afraid you saw that.''

"Of course I saw it. You're in my kitchen, aren't you?'' Susannah came around the kitchen island and walked up to the prep counter, detouring to pull a heavy steel ladle from a hook on the wall. "I saw you, too, trying to pretend that the kiss was nothing. Was it?''

Grace chewed on her lower lip for a minute, until she realized that that made her think of Tyler. She wanted to say that it had been nothing, a momentary weakness that had left her untouched when it was over. But I can't lie about everything, not if I want to be able to look these people in the eye.

"He knocked my socks off,'' she admitted. The blush that raced over her face, as Susannah laughed in delight, threatened to catch her hair on fire. "If your son runs a bar as well as he kisses, he'll have nothing to worry about.''

"But you don't want to kiss him again.''

Grace didn't want to anger Susannah, but stuck with the truth—about her intentions, at least.

"No, I don't.''

But because the part of her brain that said to hell with the consequences wouldn't shut up, she crossed her fingers behind her back.

"Next time,'' Susannah began, and Grace jumped as the

forgotten ladle clanged against the steel countertop, "hit him with this."

Grace gaped at her.

Susannah smiled.

"My boy can be pretty pushy."

And with that, Grace knew she could relax a little bit around these women. Tyler still made her tense whenever they were in the same room together, but any mother who'd hand a girl a ladle and advise her to knock her son upside the head with it clearly had a sense of humor.

A little bit later she spotted Sarah stocking extra napkins up at the bar and took the opportunity to apologize there, too. With the kindness that she was coming to expect from this family, Sarah refused the apology on the grounds that there was no way Grace could have known.

One last pep talk for everyone, a brief panic because no one could find the chalk for the daily specials board and an argument over who'd been stupid enough to leave the chalk box in the beer cooler, and they were ready for anything.

At 5:00 p.m., Tyler's Bar & Grill officially opened for business.

Three

Toward the end of her first week at Tyler's Bar & Grill, Grace admitted to herself that the one possible turn of events that she hadn't allowed herself to think of was failure.

The average dinner customer might know the Haley Group, the eleven variously styled restaurants owned by Grace's family, as a string of fabulously successful businesses. But Grace knew from experience how tough it was to open a restaurant and that even with the financial backing and publicity connections her family provided, each restaurant took time to find its crowd and prove itself stable enough to remain in business. She also knew that most independently owned establishments folded in six months.

Catching Tyler's eye from the wait station at the end of the bar and calling out her drink order, she realized she shouldn't have worried.

Apparently the man did everything well. And had personally invited everyone in a ten-block radius.

''Two pints of Bass, a Ketel One and tonic with a twist, and a very dirty martini, for the best waitress I've got." Tyler repeated the order back to her with a wink as he set the drinks on her tray.

"I'm the *only* waitress you've got, Tyler. Your sister just told me that she's a civil engineer. I had to ask her what that was." She looked to where Addy moved through the dining room, weaving between tables with one of the enormous food trays propped on her shoulder like a pro. "She goes back to designing new neighborhoods on Monday."

"Isn't she great?"

"Terrific," she agreed, thinking that her mother wouldn't cancel a manicure to help her daughter. Whereas Tyler's entire family had taken the week off to help him, without his even asking and it looked like Sarah and her mother would be sticking around on a semi-permanent basis. "But if even half this many people continue to show up daily, we're going to need another server on the floor, and Sarah's happy washing dishes."

"Not to mention stitching up dogs and cats and hamsters."

Grace blinked in confusion for a moment before figuring out how the conversation had drifted to house pets. "You mean, she's a vet?"

"Veterinary student, last term. She's completing her internship at a clinic downtown."

"Even better. But we're still going to need more help. Did you put an ad in the paper saying 'free beer' or something?"

"Nah, most of these people are just good friends who hope I stay in business long enough for them to talk me out of a free meal." He winked at her and called to a red-cheeked man at the far end of the bar, waving a twenty for his attention, "Keep your pants on, Benny. Can't you see I'm trying to make time with my waitress here?" As she blushed, he smiled wider and flicked the tip of her nose gently with his finger. "Thanks for worrying about me, darlin'. I've got some new help coming on Monday, promise."

Then he strolled off to the opposite end of the bar and poured Benny his Chardonnay, taking drink orders and chatting up his customers with an ease that hid the half-dozen things he managed to do at one time.

"I'm not worried about you, you jerk," she muttered as she pulled her tray off the bar and balanced it on her left hand. "I'm the one who's stuck serving all of these people." She looked out over the crowd. Nearly every table was full and the bar area was standing room only. She made her way to table six, a two-top up against the wall, dropping the two Bass off at a larger group along the way, and smiled cheerfully at the couple holding hands across the table.

"Here you are. And a very dirty martini for you, sir. Are you two ready to order or do you need another minute?"

They were ready to order, and Grace assured them that they would indeed be very happy with both the Greek Chicken Wrap and the Chicken Vesuvio. In fact, every dish she served from the kitchen looked delicious.

Before she stepped away from the table, the man asked her, "How's the boss treating you?" He was very eye-catching, with gray-shot blond hair pulled back into a silky ponytail and several days worth of stubble on his face. She thought of pirates and called herself silly.

"Like your typical slave-driver," she said with a wink to them both. Even before Tyler had mentioned it to her, she'd figured out that just about everyone who walked in the door knew him somehow. The man obviously did not lack for friends. Or female companionship, based on the number of women flirting outrageously with him at the bar. "How do you know Tyler?"

The man snorted. "He was the best damn employee I ever had." The redheaded woman seated across from him nodded her agreement with mirthful eyes. "At least, before he got this damn fool idea in his head. Opening his own restaurant. Ungrateful brat."

The redhead burst into outright laughter and tugged sharply on his hand. "Don't be such a curmudgeon, Richard." To Grace she said, "My husband is just mad that Tyler wouldn't let him invest in this place after he quit working for us."

"Was Tyler your bartender?" Grace asked the man, Richard, politely.

"Bartender? For about three days, he was." At her look of perplexity, he continued, "He couldn't have worked more than a couple of shifts at my joint, I hadn't even met the boy yet when he came marching into my office one day, demanding to run the place." He smiled with pleasure at the memory. "Told me that my manager was robbing me blind and that if I gave him her job, he'd straighten out the books, double my profit margin and triple my clientele."

"And?" Grace asked, fascinated in spite of herself by this glimpse into the character of the man behind the bar she was finding more appealing the more she knew him.

"He did it all." Richard shook his head. "Everything except triple the crowd. He pointed out that that would be beyond my fire capacity for the joint, and then he talked me into adding another room on."

"Smart guy." Richard's wife stated the obvious. "We miss him."

"Stupid boy," Richard said and shook his head. "Took him an extra two years to open this place because he was too stubborn to take us on as backers."

Grace grinned. "Some people just have to do it all themselves, don't they? You'd better come in as often as you can, then, to make sure he doesn't go under before Christmas."

Richard's shout of laughter caused heads to turn all over the room, including Tyler's, to whom he called, "Looks like you've got a real saleswoman over here, Tyler. I may have to steal her from you."

"And I might have to cut you off, old man," Tyler shouted back to general laughter as Grace rushed off to put in her food order.

Fifteen minutes later, when she was back at the bar for yet another round of drinks, Tyler waved her in closer so he could shout in her ear.

"If you're not in the weeds, I could use a hand with some glass-washing back here."

"Yeah, right," she said, eyeing the narrow walkway behind the bar with suspicion. There wasn't room for two people to work back there without them constantly bumping up against each other.

"I'm serious, Grace. The automatic washer comes in next week, but right now I'm doing them by hand, and with no bar back tonight, I'm not keeping up."

She scanned her tables and decided they all looked happy and occupied with their meals. It was late enough in the evening that walk-ins were slowing down, and Addy could probably handle the floor for a few minutes.

"We'll be serving martinis in paper cups soon, Grace. Please."

"Fine." She knew she sounded ungracious, but she had her hands full already. Then she ducked through the cutout section of the bar, her tray of empties on the bar preventing her from lifting the flap of counter, and discovered the extent of the disaster.

Red wineglasses, white wineglasses, steins, pints, rocks glasses, highballs, shots and flutes. Glasses piled on the counter next to the three-compartment sink, stacked on the floor, and cluttering up the tops of coolers. She was surprised there was a single clean drinking vessel left in the house.

"'Not keeping up'? Did you learn your task management skills in Pooh Corner?" She skewered Tyler with a look.

"Don't even start that," he snapped, but then had the grace to look sheepish. "Okay. So I might have understated the problem."

"I'll say." She flipped the switch that started the brushes spinning and said goodbye to her manicure.

For fifteen minutes she sweated and splashed and scrubbed her way through what felt like, and very well might have been, five hundred dirty glasses. Plunging each glass repeatedly down onto one of the spinning brushes in the sink of hot, soapy water, dunking the glass into the sink of clean, hot water tinged blue with disinfectant, and finally dipping it in the last sink of cold water to rinse. When she came across the glass someone had been using as an ashtray, she cursed Tyler under her breath.

When she realized she'd washed the wineglasses from a table of neighborhood office assistants and hadn't managed to remove all of the lipstick from any of them, necessitating a second trip through the cycle, she planned his death.

In several slow, excruciating scenarios. Most involving sharp objects being inserted beneath his fingernails.

She pulled the plugs to let the dirty liquid drain from the sinks before she refilled them with fresh water, and felt Tyler move behind her again. He'd done so a number of times already as she'd washed glasses, each time brushing past her with a minimum of contact. A very professional manner that didn't keep her from being extra aware of his movements behind the bar. She swore she could feel the heat radiating off his body when he paused behind her and rested a hand lightly on her hip for a moment, talking to the customer at the bar directly in front of her.

She ignored him and thought with pleasure of the end of her shift. For the first time in a month, she wouldn't be going home to the dubious pleasure of her room at the Sherradin Hotel.

When she'd come into work this evening, Tyler had again asked her to fill out her as-yet-uncompleted paperwork. Although she'd been surprised he hadn't reminded her of it before this, she'd still panicked at the question and blurted the first words that came into her head, cursing herself for repeating her original pathetic excuse.

"I'm so sorry, Tyler. I left my wallet back at the hotel room."

"Your hotel room?" he'd asked sharply. She was certain he didn't buy her lie for a second. "Where are you staying?"

"At the Sherradin Hotel over on Broadway" she'd said, and flinched at the anger that bloomed over his face in an instant.

"Are you an idiot? Do you know what kind of a place that is?" His voice had been loud, booming throughout the room. His eyes, which she'd once thought of as being like dark, starlit water, had been hard and jabbed at her like wrought-iron spikes. "Most of the people staying at that place are renting a room by the hour, whether they're hooking or dealing. What the hell are you doing there?"

Gathering her pride around her like a tattered shield, Grace had answered him calmly.

"It's cheap and the door has a lock."

"A lock? At the Sherradin, you'd better wedge a chair under the doorknob before you go to sleep."

"I do," she'd said truthfully.

At her short answer, he'd stopped and stared at her, flexing his hands on the smooth varnish of the bar like a man looking for something to strangle. Pride alone had kept her looking evenly back at him. She might be embarrassed to be living in a room at a hotel patronized almost exclusively by prostitutes and drug dealers, but she'd be damned if she'd be ashamed of it.

After thirty seconds and a short, pithy curse, Tyler strode to the phone and started punching in numbers with stiff fingers.

"Sarah, it's Tyler. I need a favor from you, darlin'. Can you go over to the Sherradin Hotel on Broadway before you come in here?" He let out a short bark of laughter at the woman's response. "No, not me. You'll be meeting Grace." He looked over to where Grace sat stiff-backed at the bar and grimaced. "That's exactly what I said when she told me where she was staying. I was hoping you could meet her over there in ten minutes, help her pack her bags and bring everything back here. We'll figure out where she can stay later."

When Grace started to protest, Tyler's stare and the finger he pointed sharply at the chair next to her had her sitting without saying a word.

"Thanks, Sarah. She'll be out front." Another pause, and this time when Tyler ran his eyes over her, Grace could feel the heat in them from across the room. "Don't worry. She won't open that smart mouth to argue. Thanks again." He hung up the phone.

"I don't know what you think you're doing, but—"

"Shut up and sit down."

"I am perfectly fine at the hotel."

"Grace."

The single word had her shutting up and sitting again. Tyler let out an audible sigh and pressed his fingers against his temples, shaking his head. When she worked up the nerve to meet his eyes again, she saw that all the anger had drained out of them and a calm sympathy remained.

"Grace, when I hire someone, I like to think that they'll be able to go home and get a decent night's rest before coming back to work the next day. At that hotel, you're as likely to get your throat slit as sleep through the night. Now, Sarah's going to meet you there and you are going to check out this afternoon. We'll figure the rest out later."

To her horror, Grace felt the tears fill her eyes again. She blinked them back. The thought of not having to sleep on nerves' edge at every sound in the hallway was something she'd never thought to be so grateful for. But she wouldn't cry, damn it. She stretched a hand toward him across the bar uncertainly. She let it drop after a moment, her palm resting flat against the silken grain of the wood.

"Thank you." She hoped he could hear the sincerity in her words.

After a moment she looked down at her hand, feeling the break of the visual connection with Tyler like the sudden snapping of a taut cord. Would she ever get over the sheer presence of this man? As she watched, both of his hands came sliding over the bar to rest on top of hers, and the sudden catch of breath in her chest made it clear that, no, she might never get past this. His fingers curled around the sides of her hand to tug gently upward on her palm, pulling her hand toward his mouth.

"Don't thank me, Grace. I try to take care of the people I like. And I like you."

She felt his breath on her knuckles. Glanced up. Tyler's eyes were heavy-lidded as he watched his thumbs trace small circles on the backs of her hands. Then his eyes met hers and a slow grin slid over his face as he leaned to kiss her fingertips.

"Just get your butt back here as fast as you can."

She jerked her hand from his, turned and sprinted out the door.

When Grace had jogged up to the front of the hotel, she'd spotted Sarah at once. Her long, dark hair wasn't teased high enough to fit in this area, the makeup too subdued, the skirt too long and the blouse not nearly tight enough.

I must have stuck out like a blinking neon light, too, she thought.

"I can't believe you've been staying here, Grace. You're braver than I am, that's for sure," Sarah said as she hustled them both up to Grace's room and began a ruthless packing of her belongings.

"Are these sheets yours? I thought so. They don't look dingy enough to belong to management. And the kitchen stuff, too, right? Although not this pot, obviously. What were you supposed to cook in that? A teaspoon of soup? How on earth did you end up staying here, Grace?"

Maybe it was the concern that ran so clearly through Sarah's voice. Or maybe it was the guilt she felt, taking advantage of her help in folding up the scant contents of her closet. But either way, Grace found herself giving Tyler's sister an honest, although severely edited, account of her recent history.

"I was working for my family. We all work together, but lately they've wanted to do some things with the business that I didn't agree with." Grace folded another pair of slacks and kept her eyes cast down, watching her hands work. "And I was, um, sort of involved with someone who thought my family was right and I was crazy to fight them. The only one who agreed with me was my grandmother, but then she died. And after a little while, I couldn't take it anymore. The pressure."

She looked up and saw that Sarah was watching her without a hint of judgment in her eyes.

"So two weeks ago, I just left. Packed up what you see here and decided to vanish for a while. To try and figure things out." She blew out a breath and sat on the edge of the bare mattress. "You probably think I'm a total coward."

"What I think shouldn't matter to you, Grace. But just for the record, I don't think you're a coward at all. Sometimes you need to take a step back and look at the whole picture, and that's just what you're doing." Sarah's voice was firm as she zipped up the suitcase and took one last tour around the small room.

Satisfied that they hadn't missed anything, she grabbed Grace by the hand and tugged her off the bed.

"Now let's get out of here. Tyler will be chewing nails by the time we get back to the bar."

And that had been all that was said about Grace's history and hotel choice.

On the way back to the bar, Sarah made it clear that she'd meant her kind words when she offered up a spare bedroom in her apartment. Her roommate had recently moved out and she was in no hurry to find another one. If Grace wanted to stay there for a while, she said, they could work something out between them.

When Sarah emphasized that the arrangement would be strictly casual and wouldn't involve anything like signing a lease, Grace agreed on the spot.

Finished with her glass washing behind the bar, she gave yet another heartfelt mental thank-you to this family that was taking her in as if she were one of their own. She knew it was callous to use them like this, but she couldn't remember the last time someone had offered to take care of her. She was too used to doing it all on her own.

It took her a moment to realize that Tyler still stood behind her and that the words coming out of his mouth were about *her*.

"I pretty much picked her up off the street," he was saying, "cleaned her up, and tonight I plan on taking her home with me."

"What?" she shrieked and stood up so fast that the top of her head cracked against his chin.

"Ouch." He rubbed his chin, and was pleased to see how

quickly she rose to take his bait. "I was just saying, darlin', that—"

"Not another word," she threatened, turning and advancing on him with soapy hands ready to strangle.

"—you'd be coming home with me tonight. You know you need a place to stay."

"I'm not going home with you, you moron." She was shouting by now and it felt good. "I'm going home with your sister."

When the wave of laughter from the happily eavesdropping customers broke over her, she realized that they'd gathered quite an audience. Good-natured catcalls and comments flew her way from the men seated at the bar, their girlfriends laughing along with them.

"Man, Sarah's boyfriend isn't going to be too happy to hear that!"

"Or maybe he'll be twice as happy!"

"Get your minds out of the gutter," she scolded the collection of faces at the bar.

"Don't be mad, Gracie." Catching her off guard, Tyler wrapped his arms around her and reeled her in close to him. "You're too hard to resist." With a wolfish smile, lots of teeth and a look of hunger in his eyes, he bent his head over her and she knew he was going to kiss her in front of the entire bar.

And because she wanted him to so badly, could feel herself rising up onto her toes to lean into his kiss, could feel her legs shifting to cradle one of his thighs between hers, she panicked.

Next time, hit him with this.

Susannah's words from opening night raced through her head—along with the fleeting thought that later on she'd regret this—before she reached out blindly with one hand.

She only had a moment to realize that she'd grabbed the dirty spoon Tyler had been using to stuff olives with blue cheese and then she was rapping it sharply against his skull.

"Grace!" Addy looked shocked at the far end of the bar.

Tyler rubbed his head gingerly and grimaced as he smushed the blue cheese in his hair even more.

The crowd of onlookers had doubled in number. She could see Richard and his wife clapping hands in approval across the room.

She threw her hands in the air.

"His mother told me to do it," she announced, and decided to march out from behind the bar with whatever dignity remained intact. And she did, except for the part where she had to duck down to squeeze beneath the bar counter. She headed straight to the kitchen.

Sarah and her mother were singing along to "Under the Boardwalk" when she burst through the doors. Sarah was sending the last of the big soup pots through the dishwasher and Susannah was wiping down a counter. They both looked up when they heard the saloon-style doors slam against the wall.

"I had to do it."

"Do what?" Sarah called.

Susannah was already smiling.

"I had to hit him upside the head. With a spoon."

Tyler's mother just grinned peacefully as Sarah pelted the both of them with questions. "I knew you would."

Her feet might never recover.

Grace decided that it had definitely been years since she'd worked a full schedule as a server. She propped her feet up on a chair across the aisle and dug into the plate of pasta balanced on her lap. Susannah had insisted on making her a plate when she realized that Grace hadn't had time to eat before her shift, or had a spare five minutes during it, either. They'd finally closed the kitchen at ten o'clock, although the bar would stay open until 2:00 a.m. But without food that needed to be served, Tyler could handle the customers at the bar and she could sit for the first time in eight hours.

At a table in the back of the room, she spread out with her dinner and her paperwork. She totaled up her checks and credit card receipts and counted out her cash, in between bites of rigatoni in a creamy tomato sauce.

By the time she double-checked her math, she had cleaned her plate.

All in all, it hadn't been a bad night. Not as much as she used to spend on a pair of shoes, in her old life, but enough to make a start on paying rent to Sarah. Besides, Grace thought, she was embarrassed to admit, even to herself, that she'd ever spent three hundred dollars on a pair of shoes.

"Are you making out okay here? Cash-wise, I mean."

She looked up to find Tyler standing over her. The bar was still noisy enough that she hadn't heard him walk up.

"Pretty well, actually. Your friends are good tippers."

"Yeah, well, they like you, too. Half the people who've been here tell me they'll only come back as long as I manage to hang on to you."

She didn't want to meet his eyes, so she focused on gathering up her paperwork. Stuffing her checks and receipts on one side of her order book and the balance of her cash total on the other, she clapped the book closed and passed it to him over her shoulder.

When he bopped her on the head with it, she craned her neck to glare at him in irritation. Then she remembered what he'd told her earlier when he sent his sister home and immediately felt guilty.

"Do you need me to stock something for you?" she asked. She was, after all, getting paid to work this late. "That's what I'm here for."

She couldn't tell if he was irritated or just tired when he spoke.

"Take a break, Grace. We can stock later. I was just checking to see if you wanted a drink. You get one on the house after each shift, and seeing how rough tonight was, I'll even break out the champagne if you want."

I am such a jerk. "Thanks, but I think I'll stick with coffee."

"Let me know if you change your mind." He strolled back to the bar, a bar towel tucked in his back pocket and red wine staining his left sleeve. It had been a long night for both of them.

And it was just the two of them left working. Tyler had sent his sisters and his mother home shortly after the kitchen closed. When Grace had started to protest at being left by herself with him, he'd pulled her aside so that his family couldn't hear him.

"I want them to go home, Grace. They've been spending too much time here. Addy's got a two-year-old at home. Sarah's working at the clinic before coming back here and—"

"Stop." She surprised herself by putting a finger up to his lips. "Send them home. We'll be fine."

The look of relief on his face showed her how badly he felt about relying on his family to help him out. When he hugged her, it was as a friend, and she squeezed him back without reservation.

"Thank you." He held her at arm's length and seemed to struggle to look solemn. "I promise I won't flirt with you. Not even a little bit."

"Yeah, right." She'd scoffed automatically.

"Okay, maybe just a little bit. I'm only human, darlin'."

But she trusted him not to make things difficult for her. Something about a man growing up with so many women in his family, particularly such strong-minded, outspoken women, made her comfortable with working with him until the small hours of the morning.

Then there was that part of her that *wanted* him to make things difficult for her.

Her mind kept on straying back to that one kiss in his office and the way her stomach had clenched behind the bar when he'd pulled her close again. She'd caught herself mindlessly staring into space more than once since then, unable to recall what she was doing and far too conscious of the heat pooling deliciously in her belly, remembering his kiss.

If only he didn't have such a mouth on him. Every time she looked at him she imagined it pressed fiercely against her own. She could feel the way the corner of the door frame would have edged sharply into her back if he'd continued to kiss her in the office, backing her up against the wall, and pressing her hands above her head, where they couldn't push him away.

And she wouldn't really want to.

Grace realized with a start that she was doing it again. Fantasizing about her boss. The boss she was lying to daily, even if only by what she didn't say to him. She knew she couldn't afford that kind of complication in her life right now and vowed to stop it from that moment on.

Closing time, and the ability to go hide at Sarah's apartment, never seemed so far away.

The hours passed quickly enough though, between her side work and stocking for the next day's business. Before she knew it, they were saying goodbye to the last customers of the night and Tyler was locking the door behind them.

Most of the lights at the rear of the restaurant were shut off, the ones up front dim enough to cloak the whole room in an aura of peaceful calm. She wiped down the last of the tables and straightened, arching her back in an effort to work out some of the kinks. Tyler was rummaging around behind the bar, so she felt inconspicuous enough to bend over and do a few toe-touches, stretching out her muscles. When she heard him walking toward her, she stood again quickly and reached for a chair to upend on the nearest table.

"Leave it, Grace. I've got a busboy who can come in tomorrow. He'll finish up here." She saw that he held the previously offered bottle of champagne in one hand and a pair of plastic cups in the other. At her look, he explained, "I didn't want either of us to have to wash another damn glass."

She smiled in appreciation. "Thanks. But I think I'm too tired for champagne."

He walked over to a table, set down the bottle and cups, and pulled out two chairs side by side. When he looked at her, she read nothing but tired appreciation in his gaze.

"Come sit with me, Grace. It's been one hell of a day, but after a week of being open, I'm starting to think we're going to pull it off. Surely that deserves one celebratory drink."

She wavered and was sure he could read the indecision in her eyes.

"Have I seriously hit on you once in the last few days?"

"No." She had to admit that, and repressed the thought that she'd been disappointed.

"See? And tonight I'm too wiped out to flirt even. I'm totally harmless."

"I doubt that," she muttered loud enough for him to hear and chuckle at. Then she gave in and sat next to him. When he poured her a cup of champagne, she accepted it with gratitude.

"Here's to surviving the grand opening and our first crazy week." Tyler lifted his cup and she clinked her plastic cup dully against his. "You busted your butt working tonight, darlin'. I appreciate that."

She felt the champagne she sipped burst in sharply fruited bubbles on her tongue, before tilting her head back and letting the cool liquid trickle slowly down her throat. She brought her gaze back to his and found his eyes on her, not quite as dulled now.

Safer to keep talking.

"It was hardly just me." She waved a hand in a tired circle, encompassing the whole room. "Your family work at least as hard as I do, and you put in more time than all of us."

"Yeah, well, this is my baby." He closed his eyes for a moment and she felt free to stare at him for once. He looked tired. Tired, but still strong, as if he could jump up and work another twelve-hour shift if that's what it took to run his business. Something about that determination made her want to know more about this man.

"Have you always wanted to own a restaurant?" The quietness made it easy to ask personal questions. Like trading secrets in the dark at a grade-school sleepover.

His hands where they rested on the chair arms were limp with relaxation. His voice when he spoke was surprisingly clear.

"Sometimes it feels like it." He laughed and sat up straight before stretching hugely in his chair. "But no, I didn't know what I wanted. I fell into the business by accident long before I figured out that it's what I love." He sipped champagne out of the plastic cup and seemed to think for a while before looking at her. "Are you and your dad close?"

"No." Quiet memories, so fuzzy with time as to contain almost nothing more than a feeling of warmth and a crisp smell she thought might have been her father's cologne. "He died when I was very young."

"I didn't know that." She was glad that he didn't apologize or say any of the stupid things most people came up with in an effort to comfort her for a twenty-some-year-old loss. His next words made it clear why. "Mine, too." He was gazing at his hands now as he spoke. "He was a jazz musician. Saxophone, mostly. My mom has a couple of recordings he worked on, background stuff. Not much. When I was about seventeen, I looked old for my age and I started sneaking into clubs. Blues and jazz clubs." He laughed a little and shook his head, eyes distant. "I told myself it was because I could drink beer, feel tough, get in a little trouble. But I think I was mostly just trying to remember what it felt like to hear my dad play."

He shook his head again. "After a few years I ended up working at a couple of my regular hangouts. Started out bussing tables and worked my way up. Eventually, even my boss pointed out to me that I should be running my own place. I think I was just working up the nerve."

"And now you're here," she said, pleased with the neatness of his story, but also feeling a vague jealousy that his business had such a personal meaning to him. She'd felt that way herself, before, although everyone left in her family seemed to think she was crazy for doing so.

"Well, almost here." He sank back into his chair and closed his eyes again. "If everything goes according to plan, in a year or two I'll punch out the side and add on a second room so I can have live music on the weekends."

And you can feel your dad here all the time. But she didn't say the words out loud. Just cleared her throat and asked him, "And you never wanted a partner? You know, someone to share the workload?"

"I had one, once."

She knew she was prying, but couldn't resist asking him, "What happened?"

His eyes were still shut, but she saw him grimace briefly. "It turned out that while I thought we were planning a business to run together for the rest of our lives, she was looking to open a trendy hotspot that we could sell off to some restaurant conglomerate six months later. Needless to say, she wasn't thrilled with my plan, or with me, so she dissolved the partnership, you might say."

"Ouch. Sorry."

"Hey, she returned the ring. That was nice." He tilted his head toward her and opened his eyes long enough to wink at her. "Besides, it reminded me to focus on what's important. Making a success out of this place."

"There's not a doubt in my mind that'll happen. How could it not, the way you kill yourself working around here?"

His next words made her jump.

"I haven't been working so hard that I didn't notice you taking charge a number of times, little Miss I'm Just A Waitress."

Where his voice was clear, hers squeaked. "What do you mean?"

He glanced at her, eyes dull with tiredness. "Wasn't it you I saw sending Sarah off to the kitchen on day one and bringing Maxie out to bus tables and fill water glasses?"

"Sarah was so scared she kept on dropping drinks on her customers," she answered defensively. "And Maxie was going stir-crazy in the kitchen."

"And was it you I heard that night, comp'ing the entrees for the couple at table ten?"

"That was directly related to Sarah's problem with the drinks." She bit her lip. "Although I probably should have run it by you first."

"And the two new dishes added to the daily specials board?" By now, Tyler had sat up and his eyes glinted at her.

"I just suggested to your mother that we might want to expand the options for our vegetarian diners." The magnitude of the changes she'd made during the chaos of the past week, without consulting her boss on any of them, had her cringing now. "Your mom was the one to decide we should go ahead and add the dishes tonight." His raised eyebrow drew the rest out of her. "I suggested that we wait and change the menu tomorrow."

Good Lord, she berated herself, if this is the best you can do pretending to be a waitress, you might as well quit now. Why don't you just come out and tell him you're a world-class restaurateur in charge of the Haley Group?

Her guilty thoughts must have communicated themselves to him. The next words out of his mouth were the ones she cringed to hear.

"No way were you just a waitress at your last job, Gracie."

"But, really, I was," she started to protest.

"I bet you were running the place, without getting paid an extra dime to do it, and someone else was taking all the credit."

As explanations went, she reflected, that was actually fairly close to the truth, albeit on a much smaller scale. She sighed. "I think you're right." It had been Charles's job she'd done for him, the man her family had selected and groomed to marry her. The man they'd made president of the Haley Group, despite his having no real ties to her family other than the assumption that he would eventually marry Grace. "I still should have checked with you first."

"Hey." He trapped her hands on the table with one hand and grabbed her chin with the other, forcing her to face him. "When I want an employee who can't think for herself and comes running to me with problems she ought to handle on her own, I'll tell you. Got it?" His hand on her chin moved her head up and down in a nod of agreement. "You've been terrific. Got that?" He made her nod again and then moved to release her.

Grace was still blushing with pleasure at his compliments to her. She'd always made sure to let the staff of her restaurants know when they were doing an especially good job, but she hadn't realized how much she missed having someone do the same for her.

It's only human to want someone to praise you for a job well done. I just haven't had anyone around me who bothered to notice, except Grandmother, and once she became too ill...

In the middle of these thoughts, she noticed the silence of the room and then the focus of Tyler's attention on her. Her chin was still cradled in his palm and his face was only inches away from hers. The awareness she had of his mouth was overwhelming.

"My mother told me to stay away from you," he murmured, tracing his gaze over her face like a caress and brushing a hand over the top of her head. When she didn't protest as he pulled the first pin from her hair, he tugged them all out, one by one, until the weight of her hair spilled down around her shoulders. He ran his fingers through the waves to loosen them, and flexed his fingers gently against her scalp. "She said you didn't want to kiss me again."

"She's right," Grace said, even as she leaned in closer to him, narrowing the gap, her eyes drifting shut. "I don't." And it turned out that the last step was so easy, she couldn't remember why she'd been afraid of it. "I just can't seem to remember why."

His mouth was soft against hers, his lips gently welcoming her, coaxing her mouth gradually open until his tongue found hers and teased. A gentle dance of seduction that felt as calm and safe as the comfort of home.

Why his kisses should feel like home to her was a question she was beyond asking at this point. But she didn't fight it when she felt herself relaxing beneath his touch, the tension magically draining from her neck and shoulders as his fingers stroked her there. When she sighed on an arch of pleasure beneath his mouth, she didn't care that he could hear how much he affected her.

Her soft, broken sounds of pleasure, though, triggered a change in his caresses, one that had her gasping at the sudden rush of heat through her veins. His lips raced over her face, leaving heat blooming in flushed flowers everywhere he touched, until he came back to her mouth and the fierceness of his kiss, the strength in the pressure of his hand on the back of her head, arched her deeper into his kiss.

This wasn't home. It was a wild, crazy, whirlwind tour of damp jungles and sun-soaked beaches, sparkling flavors bursting in her mouth and a million sensations she'd never felt, sights she'd never seen, compressed into a kiss that exploded in her body at mach speed.

He'd let go of her hands along the way and now she found herself bracing them on his knees as she leaned across the gap between them. In a second, he'd grabbed them again and with a sharp tug, pulled her out of her seat and over to him. The kiss didn't break and it was the most natural thing in the world for her to straddle his thighs with her own, as he sat in the chair, and climb onto his lap.

Tyler groaned beneath her. "You're killing me." He pressed his face into her chest and took a deep breath. His arms wrapped around her and held her tightly to him. When he looked back up at her, his eyes were laughing. "I imagined you like this when you first walked in here and straddled that bar chair." He pulled one hand between them and traced a path down her throat, past the open neck of her blouse, stopping at the highest button. He popped it open and raised an eyebrow. "Of course, you were naked." Another pop. "In my fantasy."

"I was, was I?" For once her eyes were on a level with his and she read in them a dark desire for her that had her draping her arms languidly over his shoulders, her hands curving back to play idly in the hair at the nape of his neck. A reckless kind of power filled her as he tipped his head forward, encouraging her to let her fingers roam more widely. She danced her touch lightly over the warm skin just beneath the collar of his shirt. His hands fell to rest gently on her hips. She tipped his head up with a gentle pressure beneath his chin and raised an eyebrow at him in teasing question, "But I'm not naked now. How disappointing that must be for you."

"That can be fixed." The lightening surge of energy as he

seized her mouth was exactly what she needed to make her forget. Forget why this was wrong. Forget who she was. Who she was pretending to be.

Just let me have this right now, she begged and didn't know to whom she was pleading. Herself. Tyler. Let me have this heat, this mindless sensation. Let me just be Grace. No questions, no lies. And let me have this man.

Then words left her and she was pure driven sensation alone, swallowing his breath as she chased his mouth with her own. She bit his lip gently when he dragged his mouth away from hers for a moment, and then gasped as his tongue thrust again into her mouth. She pushed her hands frantically through his hair, grasping the strands forcefully to hold him still as she attacked his mouth.

His hands pulled at the front of her blouse, the backs of his fingers brushing her bare stomach as he tugged the tails of her shirt free and pulled the last buttons through. The air was cool on her flushed skin as he pushed the lapels of her shirt wide open, baring her silk bra. He tore his mouth from hers and pulled back, capturing her eyes with his own for one hungry moment. Then he lowered his gaze, and so did she.

She watched him as, ignoring the bra clasp, he pulled the cups of her bra down and bared her breasts. Her nipples were hard, craving his touch, as the bra lifted them, pushed them higher to his waiting mouth. He lowered his head.

Heat burst through her and an aching bloomed between her legs that was almost painful with the wanting of him. His mouth was warm and wet as his tongue stroked her, the breath he blew on her wet nipple both cold and fiercely hot at the same time.

When he trailed his fingers feather-light over the outside curve of her other breast, she cried out on the breaking wave of pleasure.

His words, when he spoke without lifting his head, broke through the haze of heat and need like a rock through a plate-glass window.

"Am I taking you home with me tonight, after all, Grace?"

Four

The last time he'd suggested it, she'd hit him on the head with a dirty spoon.

Awake now, as if from a dream, Grace imagined what she would look like if she could see herself in a mirror, and nearly groaned out loud in frustration and embarrassment. Straddling Tyler's lap in a dimly lit restaurant, shirt open, bra tugged down beneath her breasts. The picture of wanton invitation.

She wished he hadn't asked the question, had simply continued the silent seduction that would let her pretend that she was just Grace and he was just Tyler. That the rest of the world and its problems didn't exist.

But she wasn't just Grace. And she couldn't pretend that sex with anyone, even Tyler, would make her problems go away.

Sex with anyone, especially Tyler, was only going to complicate matters.

What on earth was she doing on his lap?

She realized that he was still waiting silently for her answer and dropped her forehead down to rest it wearily against his. "No, I guess you're not."

"I was afraid of that." The words were muffled against her breasts. She smiled gently although she knew he couldn't see it. The quiet was calming. She felt at rest, oddly enough, peaceful sitting half-naked across this man's lap. When he spoke again, his voice was halfheartedly hopeful.

"You're sure about that?"

This time she did laugh. "I'm afraid so."

When his thumbnail scraped swiftly down the center seam of her pants, passion flared sharply through her and she nearly fell to the floor in her backward scramble off his lap. She gained her footing awkwardly and stood, glaring at him.

He had the grace to look sheepish, until he grinned. "Just checking." He watched as she tugged self-consciously on her bra until it once again covered her breasts. "I didn't know if you were going to try to pretend again that you didn't feel anything."

Damn, the man could be annoying. "You know perfectly well that I felt something."

"Something?"

Heat. Lightning. Crashing waves and starlight. Passion and need.

The word she settled for was close enough.

"Plenty."

The crack of his laughter shot loudly through the stillness of the empty room. "Plenty, huh? Well, I guess I'll have to settle for that."

Her feeling of awkwardness grew as she fumbled with the buttons of her blouse and he simply sat there, watching her. The irritation running through her should only be directed at herself, she knew, but her voice was still sharp when she spoke.

"Appearances to the contrary, Tyler..." she began.

He shushed her. "I know. You don't normally do this kind of thing."

That stung. "Is it so obvious?" She'd been called cold before, by men who didn't appreciate her lack of interest in them.

When she'd made it plain to Charles that, despite her family's intentions, she had no desire to go to bed with him, he'd started referring to her as the Ice Queen. But cold was the last word she would use to describe how she felt around Tyler.

"Why do you think I asked if you were coming home with me?" His smile was wry as he stood and walked over to her. He stopped far enough away that she managed to keep herself from backing up a step. "I knew that if you stopped to think for a moment, you'd figure out where we were headed. And say no."

"Then why did you? Ask, I mean." Honesty compelled her to find out.

When he reached out to run a hand lightly over her hair, she didn't pull away. "Because I like you, Grace. And I want you, too. Enough to have taken you home to my bed and made love to you until the sun rose and reminded us of a new day." He paused, and she waited silently. "But I want you badly enough to want more than one night. I'm afraid that you'd wake up tomorrow feeling like you'd made a mistake, and decide to disappear.

"And that is *not* something I want."

His words frightened her.

She turned her back to him and finished buttoning her blouse. Shoving the tails ruthlessly back beneath her waistband, she considered what to do next. Tyler's footsteps echoed lightly on the quarry tile floor as he walked back behind the bar and shut off the last of the lights. In the dark, she could admit to herself that he was right.

If she'd gone home with him—

She interrupted her own thoughts. Let's be honest. If we'd finished what we started, right there on the chair in the middle of a deserted restaurant, I would have regretted it. And regretting it, might have walked away from it.

I walked away from my own family, didn't I? My so-called fiancé, even. Why on earth should Tyler be any different?

But he was, even if she refused to acknowledge why. She

couldn't have walked away from him. And that would only make things worse in the end.

She felt him approach, a physical source of warmth at her side, as he returned to her. He handed her oversize leather purse to her. She slung it over her shoulder. She still hadn't said a word to him.

"Come on. I'll walk you to Sarah's."

She nodded her assent and they left the bar together and walked home in the dark.

She'd been afraid to fall asleep.

Afraid that in her dreams she would see herself again, sliding onto his lap. Wrapping her arms around him and watching him undress her. Afraid that in her dreams, she would cover his mouth with her own and stop him from saying the words that broke the spell and instead let herself fall all the way into the ecstasy of him.

She'd been afraid of waking up and wanting him even more.

She dreamed, instead, of the walk they shared in the night.

Their footsteps on cement had sounded loud in the utter stillness of the neighborhood streets at 3:00 a.m. The arching limbs of trees overhead caused the streetlights to cast shifting shadows in the yellow light. It was strangely intimate, this wordless walk past the houses of sleeping families and people alone in their beds. When they passed a honeysuckle bush, its sweet scent resting heavily on the warm night air, he snapped off a stem of blossoms and buried his face in their bloom before passing them to her.

She inhaled and breathed in both the honeysuckle and him. The flowers would soon be gone, she knew.

In her dream, she felt his voice like a physical force surrounding her.

What happens next, Grace?

Nothing, she answered and felt an unbearable sadness. *Nothing happens next.*

As Grace tumbled out of sleep and into wakefulness, gradually becoming aware of the sun lying in stripes across her body where it shone through the blinds, higher in the sky than it ought to be, she remembered with fading dream warmth his answer to her.

Not possible. And when you change your mind, I'll be right here.

So she woke with a smile on her face. Of disbelief, admittedly, that the man could be so unbelievably arrogant, but a smile nonetheless. She couldn't remember the last time she'd done that.

She could, however, remember the last time she'd awakened and felt safe in her bed. On this morning she was incredibly grateful to feel such simple comfort again.

The night before she hadn't even turned on the lights in her new room before falling on the bed, fully dressed, and most of the way to sleep before her head hit the pillow. She rolled over now to take a look at her temporary home and her smile broadened in gladness at the sight.

The room was small, tucked under the eaves on the third story of an old house built like a clapboard castle, with turrets and all. The ceiling sloped sharply above her bed, creating an atmosphere of cozy warmth. Someone had painted the walls a butter yellow that glowed in the morning sunlight. The hardwood floors shone richly beneath scattered rag rugs and there was, wonderfully, an actual window seat built into the outside wall. A quilted cushion and several throw pillows made it an inviting place to curl up with a book and tea. Grace could picture it on a rainy day and hoped she'd be here long enough to enjoy that pleasure.

An antique-style fan whirred softly in one corner, blowing the warm morning air pleasantly throughout the room. She'd slept beneath a single cotton sheet, which she threw back now as she rolled out of bed and onto her feet. When she reached over her head in a long stretch, her fingers brushed the slope of the ceiling and she grinned.

Sarah had left her bags on top of a long, low dresser that sat tucked beneath the lowest eave. Next to it, she'd also left a note folded on top of a blue towel and facecloth.

Grace—
Hope your first night's rest was a good one. The bathroom
is down the hall on the left. Use anything you need, and
feel free to take the same liberties in the kitchen. If you
can find anything worth eating, that is.

Tyler said last night to tell you not to show your face
in the bar before 4 p.m., but to bring the stuff you need
to complete the paperwork. I'm at work, will see you at
Tyler's later.

Welcome,
Sarah

Grace sat on the edge of the dresser with a thump. How
could she have forgotten so quickly? Clearly, that hadn't been
a problem for her boss. The small matter of her registration
with the federal government as an official employee of Tyler's
Bar & Grill was still hanging over her head.

Like a guillotine, she thought morbidly.

I'll just have to figure out how to build that bridge when I
need to cross it. But right now, what I need is a shower. A
long, hot, wash the smoke out of my hair, shower. Tyler and
his paperwork can wait.

In the bathroom, she scrubbed and soaked and refused to
notice the dark chestnut roots growing in at the base of her
honey-blond hair. She'd paid a ridiculous amount of money to
have it done at a downtown salon no one in her circle visited,
on the day she'd run away. Something about the drastic change
in hair color, and the new, softer cut she'd requested, had
shifted the whole shape and feel of her face. She looked
younger, and more vulnerable, than she had in years.

Looking at herself in the mirror, she felt sure that no one
who knew her previously would recognize her, as long as they
didn't get more than a casual look. With her current lack of
funds, she'd have to wait awhile before touching up the roots,
but she didn't think anyone would notice for at least another
couple of weeks.

Thoughts of being recognized, though, had spoiled her morning as thoroughly as thoughts of the upcoming confrontation with Tyler. Pacing the kitchen in her bathrobe, she scooped some debatably dated lemon yogurt out of a carton and tried to think her way out of either of her dilemmas.

Tyler first. If only because her problems there were more concrete. No ID, no job. But how to get around that catch-22 was the question. Could she fake a mugging on her way to work? Pretend that her wallet had been stolen and hope to ride for a week or two on that story, too busy to go to the D.M.V. to get another driver's license?

But what good would that do her, really? In a week, she'd just have to come up with another story, and although Tyler might bite once or even twice, surely it was too much to expect a third time.

You know, in spy novels it's always ridiculously easy to get a fake passport or driver's license made, she thought, angrily recalling her favorite authors. They make it sound like all you need is five hundred bucks and a phone book and it's goodbye Grace Haley, hello Grace Desmond.

I bet John LeCarre has never actually been on the run in his life, or he would have realized it just isn't that easy. At least not when you're without underworld connections.

As she got dressed in an outfit nearly identical to the one from the previous evening, she settled unhappily on the mugging story as her best of several bad options. She laced up her shoes and packed her apron back in her bag after removing her tips from the night before. The money she tucked in a dresser drawer, except for a twenty-dollar bill that she put in her wallet. She trusted Sarah, and there wasn't a lock on her door here in any case. Nor could she go and deposit the money in a bank, unless she wanted to provide her family with a way to track her down.

She locked the apartment door behind her and headed down the interior stairs. On the walk home last night, she thought she'd spotted a pay phone at the corner convenience store.

Indeed, there was a phone bolted to the exterior of the brick building, and the clerk inside was more than happy to give her

change, after she bought a bottle of lemon ice tea and a copy
of the *Sun Times* and the *Tribune*. If her family had made any
announcement about her disappearance, she'd find it in one of
the two Chicago dailies.

She flipped through every page of both papers, sitting on a
curb in the parking lot, and then did it again from back to front.

Nothing.

Not a word about her disappearance for more than two weeks
in a row now.

It wasn't as if she'd expected the headlines to be blaring
Heiress Kidnapped! After all, she had left a note in plain view
on the dining room table of her penthouse condo, where anyone
coming to check on her would find it. Or her cleaning lady
would have come across it and called her family. And she'd
popped another little security blanket in the mail to her attorney, too.

But it wasn't mere ego, either, that had made her expect to
see something about her abrupt departure from the Chicago
restaurant scene in the newspapers. She was a well-known figure in the kind of circles that were regularly written up in the
society columns of the local papers. And almost three weeks
without an appearance by her at some charity function or event
hosted at one of the Haley restaurants ought to have been oc-
casion for some notice.

Shaking her head, she tucked the papers in her bag and
crossed to the pay phone.

Maybe Paul would have some answers for her.

Once again, one of Chicago's elite French chefs was less
than thrilled to be rousted from sleep at what he considered the
indecent morning hour of noon. But he was happy enough to
hear from her and more than willing to clear up the mystery
of her family's lack of public reaction.

"They what?"

She ignored the heads of passing pedestrians that turned at
her shriek and shoved more quarters in the phone as the re-
corded voice broke in for the second time.

"They say you are sick with grief over your *grandmère*,

chérie. That because she dies, you cannot…what did they say? Think straight,'' Paul explained again patiently. ''They say that you have gone off to one of those fancy hospitals for rich women with too many problems. You know, like that president's poor wife.''

''Oh, for God's sake,'' she sputtered. ''They're telling people I'm at some kind of rehab clinic? Who's going to believe that?''

''*Ma chère,* if you are not here to show them otherwise, many people will believe it.''

''What a mess.'' Grace slumped against the edge of the phone booth and stared blankly at the street in front of her. She'd thought to buy herself some time and perhaps hoped to make her family worry. Take her seriously for once.

''Indeed it is,'' Paul said sternly in her ear. She could hear his disapproval ringing down the phone line. ''But everything can be fixed, *chérie,* if you would just come home!'' His voice was booming by the final words.

''I can't, Paul.''

''Why not?''

Grace took a deep breath. She needed to share her burden with someone, and there was no one she trusted more than Paul. ''They want to sell the restaurants.''

''Who does? Which restaurants?''

''My family does, Paul. And Charles, too.'' And then the worst part of all. ''They want to sell all of the restaurants. They've already lined up a buyer for each one.''

The silence over the phone line was deafening. Paul had worked for the Haley Group restaurants since Grace's grandmother had gone into business, and she knew the news that her family wanted to break up the company would devastate him. Paul had worked in every restaurant in the corporation, as varied as the cuisines and decor and attitude might be, and looked on each one as being one of his children. For the past ten years, he had reigned as head chef at Nîce, the capstone of the Haley Group.

"Even my restaurant?" In Paul's mind, it was his kitchen, therefore his restaurant.

"Yes."

"You are certain that they meant my restaurant, too."

Grace's laugh was shaky. At least Paul would always remain the same. "I'm certain." He muttered something in French. "I don't think you ever taught me the translation for that one."

"You don't want to know, chérie. But I still do not understand. Your grandmother, she put you in control of the Haley group, yes?"

"Not exactly." Grace wondered how to explain it to this crazy, lovable Frenchman who had to have a sous chef balance his checkbook for him. "She made me the CFO and Managing Director, which means I'm in charge of all the day-to-day decision-making, but Charles is still the president. Even if he is mostly a figurehead."

The thought of how Charles had schemed his way into her family, playing on their trust in family ties that went back generations, until he'd convinced everyone that his visibility and social connections made him the prefect image-maker for the restaurant conglomeration, still made her want to stick pins in a voodoo doll.

"That boy. He does not know a pâté from a piece of…never mind. I have been thinking that you owned the Haley Group, Grace."

"A large part of it, but not all." Grace forced herself to continue speaking as if her next words didn't break her heart. "Grandmother meant to change her will, but she fell ill first. She left me fifty percent of the Haley Group. Enough that they can't sell without me, but I can't get rid of them, either."

"These troublemakers?"

Her laugh was born weakly from the sharp pain beneath her breastbone. "Yes. These troublemakers." Her custom-tailored boyfriend. Her mother. Her family. People who were supposed to be her support, her bedrock. Not her betrayers.

Family wasn't supposed to try to sell off, piece by piece, all that you had worked to put together over the years.

"Paul, I'm out of quarters here. Just keep an eye out, will you? And don't worry, before any deals are made, I think I have one last option to play." After all she'd done to hide, the next step ran against every instinct, but she needed the connection. "If there's an emergency, you can leave a message for me at a tavern uptown. It's called Tyler's."

Grace used the hours before her shift to set in motion what she feared might be a last-ditch attempt to save her restaurants from being scavenged like a corpse on the Serengeti Plain. It's funny, she thought as she waited on hold at yet another pay phone, I don't even remember when I started to think of them as mine. To feel as if each restaurant, from the flowers on the host desk to the lock on the Dumpster, belongs to me, if only because I know it so well.

But they *are* mine.

She felt pride of ownership at the thought, stronger than when she'd thought of the restaurants as belonging to her family as a whole.

But my mother and Charles don't value them as anything other than investments. They can't understand why we shouldn't just sell them off and pocket the cash. Go play in the Mediterranean for a good long while. They've never understood what it meant to Grandmother, what it means to me, to see the business she built up from a deli on State Street blossom into *this*.

I'm damned if I'll sell off her vision.

My vision.

Grace reined in her irritation at the thought of the various investment groups and individuals who wanted to purchase each Haley Group property. She imagined them as drooling, panting greyhounds at the starting line of a racetrack, moments from springing ahead and chasing down the prize. But that wasn't fair. In all likelihood, each potential buyer was completely unaware that those offering to sell off a piece of the Haley Group were not, in fact, authorized to do so.

Which sparked an idea.

Another hour and she'd drafted a list of instructions to her attorney. She would wait to send them off, hoping to find a way to settle matters with her family amicably. But if necessary, she would use whatever weapons she had to preserve her Grandmother's vision. Grace's own dream.

Charles and her mother would find they weren't the only ones who could betray blood.

Tyler's immediate grin and the casual, "Hey there, Gracie, darlin'," he tossed out upon seeing her, did nothing to blind her to the fact she was walking into the lion's den.

"How'd lunch go?" she asked. Today, Saturday, had been his first day open for lunch, although Tyler had expected it to be slow.

"Better than I expected." He finished wiping down the bar and then flicked the bar rag at a man sitting by the taps, his back to the room. "Probably helped that I had such a charming devil behind the bar." The man shook his head and waved Tyler off. Grace saw that he seemed to be reading some kind of legal document. "Grace Desmond, meet Spencer Reed, Addy's husband. The finest attorney north of the Loop."

"You're just impressed that I talked the alderman out of a liquor license in time for your grand opening," Spencer said, turning on his stool.

Tall and wiry, with curling blond hair, a wicked grin and wire-rimmed glasses that he obviously used only for reading as he peered over them at her. Grace got the impression of fair-haired Clark Kent, and understood why Addy went home with such a smile in her eyes.

"You bet I am. Doesn't do much good, opening a bar and grill, if you can't have the bar half open, along with the grill."

Introductions continued, Grace shook hands with all the sincerity she could muster, less than thrilled to find herself chatting casually with a well-known Chicago attorney. Particularly one whose eyes locked on her with calculated observation. Not suspicion, exactly. But as if he were taking a mental photograph, listing bullet points under the heading "For Further Investigation.'' She was afraid it wouldn't take him long to figure out where he'd seen her before.

The contrast with Tyler couldn't have been clearer. Spencer was the kind of man Grace was used to dealing with in her regular life. Polished. Urbane. Comfortable traveling in the upper echelon of society. And she could appreciate with a woman's eyes that he was physically attractive. But she observed him as she would an Ansel Adams photograph, with appreciation but no desire to acquire it.

Tyler made her need to own, to possess, stand up and shout out loud.

He was rough-edged, as likely to assault a woman with a knee-weakening kiss in the middle of a crowded bar as to carefully walk her home without attempting to hold her hand. He dedicated himself to pursuing his goals without rest, and worked from a strength in family that let him rely on his mother and sisters to lend a hand when disaster struck. And he cared enough about an unknown diner waitress he'd hired on the fly to make sure that she slept in a safe place.

And the fact that Tyler makes you drool doesn't factor in at all, Grace?

She was glad that Tyler chose that moment to walk to the far end of the bar. It was hard to look a man in the face when you couldn't stop yourself from picturing him naked. Then she saw the papers he held in his hand, and all pretense of serenity fled.

"Come on, let's get this over with.'' He waved her over to a seat at the end of the bar.

Grace felt light-headed and figured it was a toss-up as to whether she passed out or threw up. She knew in an instant that she could never pull off the mugging story.

The truth?

Not a chance. She might find Tyler as sexy as all get-out, but that didn't mean he wouldn't be on the phone to the newspapers as soon as he found out who she was. Any money he might be paid aside, the free publicity alone—Haley Works For Tips At Tyler's Pub—would be priceless.

Even in a best-case scenario, Grace could picture him contacting her family, because he felt sorry for her, and for them, and thought he could fix things. The man had shown distinct tendencies to take care of the women in his life, and she supposed she was one of those women now, if only as an employee.

The entire question was pointless, really. Spencer Reed sat at the other end of the bar and she wouldn't be saying a damn word in front of witnesses, particularly not that one.

So. No answer at all.

"I can't fill those papers out."

"Really. Why?" He didn't strike her as being surprised or concerned. Rather, he seemed watchful, as if she had just provided him with one of several expected responses.

"Does it matter?"

He shook his head impatiently, as if in disbelief at her stupidity. "Of course it does. Are you a criminal on the run from the law?"

She knew the question was meant to be ridiculous. "Of course not."

"There you go." His grin was encouraging. "That would be bad." He stopped for a moment and looked at her. Then he turned, poured her a cup of coffee and set it in front of her with sugar and half-and-half. "Drink this." She wrapped her hands around the solid ceramic mug. "Damn it, Grace. You always look so vulnerable. I'd probably try to help you if you'd just broken out of jail where you'd been locked up for robbing banks."

"I might have tried that, if you hadn't given me a job." She looked down into her cloudy coffee. She hadn't meant to bring up her earlier precarious position.

Silence radiated from Tyler like heat from a fire. Apparently he wanted more. She just didn't have it to give to him. "I can't fill out those papers. I can't give you a social security number, or a driver's license. I just can't." She hunched defensively over her coffee, leaning on the bar. Her hazy reflection stared back at her from the high gloss of the wood. She avoided her own eyes.

"And I can't pay you under the table." Tyler's pronouncement dropped on her with the heavy weight of finality. Grace leaned back in her chair, boneless, dropping her head back and closing her eyes. The game was up. She wondered if Sarah would want her to pack up her things today, or if she could stay one more night.

She took some comfort from the fact that at least Tyler didn't sound terribly mad at her. More regretful than anything else. Perhaps she could come back here sometime and visit.

"Grace, look at me." She owed him that much, for trying to help her. And she saw that he was truly not mad at her, saw instead a well of deep compassion tinged with sadness. "You know how important this restaurant is to me." His gaze was steady and warm and she knew he was thinking of the night before and what he'd shared about why this meant so much to him. "Important enough that I won't do anything that might hurt it, like breaking the law."

"I know." She felt suddenly ashamed of herself. "I shouldn't have even thought that you might, or put you in that position. You've made this a wonderful space, and I know you'll be successful here."

"Thank you. Coming from you, I consider that an enormous compliment." The fact that he was sincere, that he would say such a lovely thing to a woman he knew only as a recently hired waitress, made her regret even more her unfair judgments of him earlier.

Perhaps if I had more courage, I could simply tell him, right now, who I am and what I'm hiding from. But I can't do that. I couldn't bear the possibility that he might look at me and think that I was pathetic, some whiny little rich girl who didn't know what problems really were.

Tyler refilled her coffee, unnecessarily, since she'd been too nervous to do more than warm her suddenly cold hands on the mug. The uncharacteristic absent-mindedness had her looking sharply at him. His brows were drawn in and down, deepening the lines between them, and his unfocused eyes stared at nothing. He returned the coffeepot to the hot plate and leaned back against a cooler. After a minute he looked hard at her, searching for something in her face, and then glanced at Spencer, still working at the far end. His glance bounced back and forth between the two of them for a minute more before he stood, having clearly come to a decision about something.

First, to Grace, "I won't pay you under the table."

"I understand—"

He cut her off and then called down the bar, "Hey, Spence, I have a question for you. If I had an employee and I realized after a couple of months that I'd switched two digits of her social security number, am I gonna bring down the wrath of the IRS if I correct the error on the last day of the year?"

Grace held her breath and thought frantically. She could see Spencer push his glasses up and cock his head in their direction. By the time she puzzled it out in her own mind, he was already speaking.

"I'm not a tax attorney, so don't bet the house on this, Tyler. But I don't think so." Spencer shrugged. "It's not going to get you in good with your accountant, but I don't think the IRS will bother to pay attention."

"What do you say, Gracie?" Tyler challenged her, leaning on the bar with his elbows, chin propped on interlaced fingers, crowding her. "It's almost October now. Flip-flop a couple digits in your social security number, don't even tell me which ones, and you'll have until the end of the year to straighten out whatever problems you have. Of course, I'll help you out any way I can."

Stunned, she simply sat there, unable to think straight, sure there must be a catch somewhere.

"But on December thirty-first, New Year's Eve, you sign on one hundred percent, and there'll be no more hiding for you.

"Do we have a deal?"

Five

"Why are you doing this?"

She was stalling for time and Tyler understood that. That he answered her question anyway was just another sign of his generosity.

The decision to offer this way out seemed to have cheered him up somehow. He winked at her as he poured several ounces of Tullamore Dew, a fine Irish whiskey, in a snifter. "You could say it's because I like taking risks." He slid the snifter thirty feet down the bar rail without a second glance. Spencer lifted the glass in the air in a casual toast that spoke of familiarity with this method of drink delivery. "That's on the house, Spence, for your legal wisdom." A smile broke slowly over his face and she felt it like a kiss on the back of her neck that made her knees weak. "Or you could say that I'm still hoping to get into your pants, and that seems easier to accomplish if you're still around."

The coffee she'd managed to sip sputtered out of her mouth

and onto the bar. Tyler laughed delightedly. She mopped it up with a napkin.

"Ah, Grace, you're so easy to tease. It's hard for a man to resist." He grabbed one of her hands in his and stroked the back of her hand with a calloused thumb. "I was just kidding."

"Yeah, right." She shot him a dark look and ignored the chills walking steadily up her arm with each stroke of his thumb.

Another one of those lightening mood changes that kept her feeling so off balance swept over him. He turned her hand over so that her palm faced up and began intently tracing a shape on the sensitive skin there. Grace had only just figured out that he was drawing a heart, which made her breath catch, when he stopped and bent over her hand to press a single soft kiss to the center of her palm, on top of his heart.

Maybe she just wouldn't bother to breathe ever again.

His voice was low and rough when he spoke. "Or you could say that from the moment you walked in this bar, I wanted you. And that with every day that passes, every time you tug on your hair in nervousness, or give an order to my family in my restaurant, I think I care about you a little bit more."

The need for air, and space, became overwhelming. Grace found herself standing next to her bar stool, tugging to free her hand from the hold Tyler kept on it. This wasn't happening to her.

Tyler was not falling for her. That was simply not possible and she refused to accept it.

"Don't be ridiculous," she managed to gasp still pulling on her hand. "Let me go."

He released her the moment she asked, suddenly enough to make her stumble and put a hand on the bar to steady herself. The disappointment in his eyes smacked her like an accusation. Her chest was heaving with deep, oxygen-desperate breaths, as if she'd just sprinted around the block.

"Not exactly the reaction I'd hoped for," he murmured, a twisted smile on his face. "I should have stuck with just getting in your pants."

Her laugh was harsh and cracked on the high note. "Listen, Tyler, you can't—we can't—"

"Don't worry, darlin'," he interrupted. "We can pretend I never said that. Or, even better, that I was wrong."

"Wrong?"

"Yup, just wrong. Thought I was falling for you, got to know you better and figured out, nah, you and I are just meant to be friends, after all." She stared at him blankly. "Wouldn't be the first time I was wrong about that kind of thing."

She didn't know why she should feel almost offended. He was giving her exactly what she wanted. But what kind of man was he, that he could toss out those devastating words and then two seconds later write them off so casually?

Why did her heart hurt at the thought of Tyler regarding her as just a friend?

"I can't think," she said, sitting back down on the bar stool.

"First things first, Grace," he said and crossed his arms over his chest, stretching his white button-down tight across his shoulders. "Focus on the job. Do you want to keep it or not?"

Two men in dirty jeans and scoffed leather boots walked in the door and came to the bar, setting hard hats down on the wood counter. Tyler strolled to take their order, and she heard him hassle them in a friendly way about quitting early for the day. He pulled them two pints of lager and walked back to her.

"Yes." She wanted the job. Her options were nonexistent at this point, something they both knew.

"And on December thirty-first?"

She'd never planned on hiding out that long anyway.

"I'll tell you everything you want to know." *And then you'll hate me and I won't have to worry about whether or not you might have been in love with me. What a bargain.*

"It's a deal." He stuck his hand over the bar and, for the second time since they'd met, they shook on an agreement. Only somehow this time it felt as though she was cementing a deal where she lost something, not gained.

"And, um, that other matter?" She felt the heat rising from her cheeks and knew she was blushing furiously.

Tyler raised his eyebrows at her. "I'm glad you think so much of my determination. But you've got nothing to worry about." He began wiping the bar down with a clean rag. "I don't like getting shot down any more than another man would. I won't try again."

A half hour later Sarah showed up for her shift. Grace knew immediately that something was wrong. Sarah, who'd been so wonderfully supportive and friendly to her from the moment they'd met, rushed straight back to the kitchen with only a wave at Grace's called-out greeting.

When Grace followed her to the back, she found Sarah tying on her apron. At the noise of the swinging doors, the other woman pressed her hands swiftly to her eyes and wiped them dry. A quick question had her spilling out the story.

"It's silly, I know. Vets have to put dogs to sleep all the time," she said. She wrapped her arms around herself and huddled in on herself. "And Piper was old and in pain. He couldn't walk, couldn't eat. But it's just so sad."

Grace found herself weeping, surprisingly, at the thought of an old dog, tired and ready to die. "Of course it is, Sarah."

"Todd says I shouldn't let it bother me." Her sudden, guilty glance told Grace that Todd was the vet Sarah worked for, the one she was dating. "He says it doesn't help to get emotional over death. That it's a natural part of life, and my feeling sad about it doesn't help the people who are there with their pet."

"Death is a natural part of life, but so is feeling grief when someone or something dies," Grace said. The wave of fierce anger at this Todd that washed over her caught her off guard. She knew most of it came from memories of hearing similar words from her family upon her grandmother's death, and what they'd called her "excessive grief." "And if I had to put a pet to sleep, I'd want a vet who could be sad with me. Not some unfeeling, uncaring block of ice who's hardly human." She surprised herself further by reaching out and enfolding Sarah in a hug. Sarah squeezed her back and sniffled one last time before letting go.

"Todd's not like that, really. He's just better at keeping his emotions separate from his work than I am." Sarah wiped her eyes as she pulled a scrunchie out of her apron pocket and twisted her long, straight hair up on top of her head. "He's an excellent vet."

Grace made a noise of noncommittal agreement and handed Sarah a paper napkin. She would keep her mouth shut. It wasn't her place to give sisterly advice.

"Did you find everything all right at the apartment this morning? I left you a note."

"I got it." The morning seemed a lifetime ago. She smiled at the thought. "Everything was perfect. I haven't had that much hot water in weeks. I'm so grateful, Sarah, that you're letting me stay with you."

"Frankly, I don't like living by myself, too many mysterious noises in the night and all that, so you're doing me a favor, actually. Although don't tell my brother that or he'll never let me live alone again."

The mention of Tyler was like a splash in the face of dirty water from the kitchen sink.

"Tyler."

She hadn't meant to say his name out loud, certainly not with such an obvious amount of frustration in her voice.

"What did he do now?" Sarah asked as she started setting up for the night, refilling the dishwasher soap and stacking up the trays that held the dishes to the right of the sink. "When he stopped by the apartment this morning, I told him not to hassle you. That it sounded to me like you'd had plenty of trouble from men lately and didn't need him coming on to you like some ham-handed farmboy." She glanced over her shoulder at Grace. "I hope that was okay."

It was probably harmless, but Grace was curious as to what Tyler had been told. "What exactly did you say to him?"

Sarah bit her lip and wiped her hands dry on her apron. "Not very much. Just that I thought you'd been involved with some guy who didn't treat you very well. I didn't mean to break a confidence, I just thought he might be better off knowing."

Grace guessed that it was Sarah's own problems with her love life that had caused her to focus on that part of the limited explanation she'd been given at the hotel, which was fine. And Sarah's edited version also explained why Tyler was being so nice to her, letting her keep working. He thought she was hiding from nothing more serious than a bad relationship.

Another idea gave her pause. A bad relationship? Or an abusive one?

If Tyler thought a woman was hiding from an abusive boyfriend, his protective instincts might go into overdrive. And, she thought further, with pain, if he was attracted at all to a woman like that, learning that she was trying to escape from a situation like that might be enough to make him want to take care of her. And that might be enough to make him think he was falling for her.

"Grace?" Sarah was still looking at her as if worried she'd made a mistake.

"Don't worry. I was just curious," Grace reassured her. It's just that I'm losing my mind over here. I can't decide if I'm happy or sad, angry or pleased, about any damn thing and your brother seems to be tied up in the middle of it all somehow. Sarah still looked concerned, so she fibbed, "I assumed you'd tell him sooner or later."

"What did he do, anyway? You sounded… Hmm…" Sarah chose her word carefully. "Frustrated."

"Oh, he just told me he was falling for me." Annoyed again, Grace grabbed a box of red-and-green cocktail straws and began ruthlessly shoving them into side compartments of a napkin holder. She waited for the shriek of disbelief.

"Wow." Sarah's voice came as a low, awed mutter from somewhere behind her. "Big brother's in love." The kitchen doors squeaked on their hinges and then thwapped back and forth against each other. "Hey, Mom, Tyler's in love with Grace."

"He is, is he?"

"Of course he's not," Grace snapped, stomping her foot as she turned around. This was worse than getting caught kissing the man in front of his mother. "He simply said he thought he might be. I told him he was crazy. Then we straightened out some other business and he decided that he wasn't after all."

"Right," Sarah said decisively. "He's trying not to scare you off. Good plan."

"Good plan? He's insane," Grace retorted, then looked apologetically at Tyler's mother.

Susannah had carried an enormous bowl of tomatoes from the restaurant-size refrigerator and now began to chop them on the island.

"My husband Michael told me that he loved me the night we met."

Both younger women listened, Sarah smiling as she heard again what was obviously a treasured family story.

"He was a saxophone player in a blues band playing at a club my girlfriends and I had snuck into. I was seventeen. At the band's first break, Michael came over to our table and told me I was the most beautiful girl he'd ever seen." Susannah shook her head. "I looked pretty good that night."

"You're still the most beautiful woman I know, Mom."

"Hush. Flattery will not get you a slice of the key lime pie I'm making tonight." Susannah wrinkled her nose at her daughter. "Let's just say he was pretty charming and handsome as sin besides. He sat next to me and we started talking. When the band went back onstage after their break, he stayed with me and we just kept talking. We sat there until the bar closed, and my friends were begging me to leave, so he walked me to the door of the club and kissed me for the first time. Then he told me he was in love with me."

"What did you say?" Grace asked after five seconds during which she made a vain effort not to be charmed by the story.

"Say? Nothing." Susannah laughed. "I smacked him in the face. I thought he was making fun of me. I didn't believe him until he kept showing up at my house every night for weeks."

"That's my mom. Always the romantic." Maxie strolled through the kitchen, yanking a baseball hat off her spiky mop of cropped curls, apparently having caught the tail end of the story.

"Be quiet." Susannah threw a ripe tomato at her youngest's head, who caught it one-handed and bit into it like it was an apple. "Someday you'll fall in love and find out that it's not all light and music. Love can be frightening, if you're not ready for it."

"No thanks. I'll pass." Maxie took another bite. "Besides, who's in love? Not Sarah and Dr. Defective, please."

"Max!" Sarah shouted and threw a dirty wet dishtowel at her sister's head while Grace choked back laughter unsuccessfully. Max seemed to inspire a lot of thrown objects. Sarah gave her a dirty look for laughing, and struck back below the belt. "Tyler's in love with Grace."

"Holy—" Max cut herself off with a glance at her mother, whose face clearly forbade cursing in the kitchen "—cow. Really?"

"No, not really," Grace answered firmly. "He just thought he might be. But now he isn't."

"What?"

"Don't look at me like you're the one who's confused." She was finished with the cocktail straws and slammed the box back onto the shelf. "You're not the one he's saying all this nonsense to."

Max scrunched her face up and was silent for a moment. A moment that didn't last.

"So you're not in love with him?"

"I can't be." The answer was automatic. She could feel the other women in the room watching her speculatively. She didn't notice when she repeated her answer.

"Can, can't. Should, shouldn't. That isn't the question." Susannah had come out from behind the prep counter to stand by Grace. Now she laid a hand on Grace's arm, as if to hold her in place. "My son, whatever he says, cares about you. The question is, how much do you care about him?"

Her vision blurred as the tears rose and she pressed her lips together. If she didn't answer, then none of it was true. She could retain some small hold on her sanity if she simply didn't answer the question. She felt Susannah's hand grip her arm tightly for a moment, comforting her.

"Such a sad girl." The older woman's hand brushed softly against her hair before dropping to her shoulder and patting gently. "I'm afraid you'll hurt my boy very badly."

Grace shook her head. *I don't want to hurt anybody,* she wanted to cry out. *I'm just trying to find my way out of all these disasters.* She tilted her head back and blinked rapidly until the tears dried. She wouldn't break down in front of these women, no matter how kind they were. When she stood straight again, Max and Sarah had moved off to another part of the kitchen. She took a deep breath and let it out slowly. Smiled like brittle glass and said to Susannah, "Everything will be fine."

A moment. Then Susannah nodded in understanding and sighed herself, before physically shaking off the mood with her whole body. "So, maybe it's better this way. You won't fall in love with him. He will not fall in love with you. There are still limes that need to be squeezed for pie. Come help me, and you can have the first piece."

"Hey!" Maxie's shout from the dish room was outraged.

And with that, the Saturday night shift at Tyler's began, all the women working smoothly together as if in agreement that nothing more need be said about preshift matters. When Grace wiped down the menus in preparation for the dinner rush and noticed that at some time during the day, Tyler had reprinted the paper inserts to include the two vegetarian dishes she'd suggested earlier, she managed to feel only an employee's pride at making a contribution.

When she called out her first drink order of the night at the bar and Tyler smiled and teased her like a sister, she told herself she was glad he could move on. They both could.

She was even able to laugh with everyone else at the bar when a heavily made-up blonde performed impromptu karaoke, singing along with Ella Fitzgerald on "Let's Do It" and gesturing boldly at Tyler.

Birds do it, bees do it,
Even educated fleas do it,
Let's do it, let's fall in love.

"I need a Heineken, two Lites and a diet, please," Grace called from the wait station at the end of the song. She shoved her ticket in the metal coil that served to hold it for the bartender to ring up. "Educated fleas, my ass."

"Jealous?" Tyler handed the ticket back to her after ringing up the round. "I thought she did pretty good myself."

"She was great," Grace said in a voice sweet enough to make a diabetic go into shock, "if you go for the obvious type."

"Better obvious than oblivious," he shot back just as sweetly.

She snatched her tray off the bar and walked away before giving in to the temptation to use a rude hand gesture.

At home that night, in her little room under the eaves, Grace stripped off her clothes, threw them in the corner and climbed into bed. The moon shining through the blinds cast thin stripes of pale light across her ceiling. She told herself that it had been another good night, a steady, happy crowd at the bar and full tables on the floor all night long. She'd made good money waiting on her customers, and things were running much more smoothly these days.

That she'd been disappointed when Tyler had called a cab to drive her the short distance to Sarah's apartment, saying he had paperwork he wanted to get done, was a weakness she would overcome soon enough. Making a work relationship into something more personal was inadvisable. And unprofessional.

You wanted the job, and you got it, she told herself in the cool dark. Don't be foolish and keep wanting something more.

Something that you can't have.

She closed her eyes and concentrated on relaxing tense muscles, tightening each individual fiber in her body and then releasing it back to a state of complete relaxation. She would unwind and sleep, and tomorrow she would be able to go through her day without the constant emotional stress of the recent summer. It would be lovely to be on an even keel again.

One week later she was crawling the walls and seriously considering climbing the Sears Tower with her bare hands and no net. Just to relieve a little of the frustration and bottled-up energy she had.

Hey, that French guy did it a while ago, blocked traffic in the Loop for hours, she thought. She was wiping down tables in the dining room and watching a trio of office women on a two-martini-or-more lunch practically fling themselves over the bar at Tyler. Climbing one hundred and twenty stories couldn't be any more draining than watching *this* every day.

Tyler and his harem of hopefuls.

To be fair, she reminded herself, Tyler hadn't actually taken any of them up on their increasingly blatant offers, as far as she knew. But did he have to be so goddamn charming?

The man would flirt with a fence post, I swear.

Grace dismissed the niggling thought that some of her irritation might arise from the fact that Tyler seemed to be turning that flirtatious charm on every woman who set foot in the bar, except for her.

She dragged a chair roughly from the middle of an aisle and slammed it into place at the proper table. She couldn't count how many times each night she found little, folded-up napkins behind the bar, all with women's names and telephone numbers scribbled on them. Some had more explicit invitations on them and most had the inevitable lipstick-print kiss.

And that man, with his smiles and his shrugs and his words about not wanting to hurt the women's feelings by throwing the napkins away while they might see him do it.

When Grace had replied that to hurt most of these women's feelings, you'd have to kick them rather hard in the rear because their heads had obviously already been affected by their cocktails, Tyler had simply laughed.

Even with these three at the bar, one of whom looked ready

to slide off her bar stool into a liquid puddle on the floor, he was at his most charming, winking and smiling like a politician.

When he finally came down to the wait station to collect her checks and money from lunch, Grace was already untying her apron, ready to walk out the door.

"Don't tell me you're abandoning me to those three?"

Grace flicked a dismissive glance at the three beauties at the other end of the bar. The one in the middle had her fingers hooked in her mouth in what Grace hoped was an attempt to whistle Tyler back down to them. "Looks like they're having a grand old time. You should be proud."

"Grace, please." Tyler grabbed her hand and pulled it to his chest. "They're blitzed, they've been coming here for lunch every day for a week, and now the dark-haired one is threatening to make me judge a lingerie contest between the three of them."

"A lingerie contest?" Grace tried to keep the grin she felt from creeping onto her face as she realized that Tyler's desperation was very much real.

"All I know is that they said something about demi versus full cup," he said. "And then I ran away. Come on, Gracie, help me out here. In another ten minutes I'm going to have a bunch of half-naked women sitting at my bar."

"Big John and Ted would be thrilled," she drawled, referring to the two construction workers who came in every day after work for a beer. Then she took pity on him and ducked beneath the countertop to join him behind the bar. She turned sideways to scoot past Tyler in the narrow space and was surprised to feel his hands wrap themselves around her waist.

He bent over her and buried his face against her neck for one long moment while she stood frozen. In a week, he hadn't touched her, except by accident, and now she could feel his lips pressed against her neck, not kissing her, but just resting there softly. When he lifted his head, brushed his lips across her cheekbone and ear, his breath washing against her skin warmly, she shivered, and knew he felt it.

"Just in case you have to pretend to be my girlfriend," he

whispered in her ear. His hands where they rested on her waist were warm. His fingers flexed gently. "To save me."

She wedged her hands between them and shoved him away with a sharp push to his chest, sure that he was making fun of her. Wondered how long she would remember the feel of the flat planes and smooth ridges of his body beneath her hands.

"I wouldn't pretend to be your girlfriend," she said sweetly, "to save you from a pack of ravening wolves."

"Hopefully the wolves wouldn't be trying to get me into bed." Tyler threw up his hands in surrender before she made up her mind to take a swing at him. "Just make them go away, Gracie, please."

"Relax, Mr. Magnetism. I'll have them out of here faster than you can say, 'Check, please.'" When the wicked impulse slid over her she didn't resist. Rising on tiptoe, she pressed her entire body against his, until she could feel his shirt buttons pressing through her blouse against her breasts.

She coiled an arm slowly around Tyler's neck and pressed a palm against the back of his head, holding him in place. Lifting her mouth to his ear, she exhaled softly and then whispered, "I'll have them back for lunch next week, too. And believe me—" she walked the fingers of her free hand silkily up his arm "—they'll never hit on you again."

She scraped her fingernails gently across the side of his face and walked to the other end of the bar.

Tyler felt as though he'd been punched in the gut.

He rubbed his stomach reflexively and watched Grace saunter down to where the three women sat. "Damn," he muttered, and raised a hand to his face to scrub away the ghost of a soft mouth brushing with the barest touch against him. He was a grade-school boy with an uncontrollable erection in math class.

Totally inappropriate, potentially humiliating, and absolutely nothing he could do about it.

He yanked free the bar rag that was tucked in the back of his belt and switched it to the front of his pants, attempting some artful draping, and hoped that thoughts of baseball would help.

Where the hell had *that* come from?

Okay, he probably shouldn't have teased Grace like that about pretending to be his girlfriend. And he knew the moment he set hands on her that that was not a good idea at all. He'd felt the sudden tightening of her stomach muscles beneath his fingers and had to fight himself to leave his hands sitting in place on her small waist. The urge to skim them up the sides of her rib cage, brushing against the sides of her breasts, had been near irresistible.

But he'd promised her that he'd back off.

And I've done it, haven't I? Even if it's damn near killed me to watch her walk out that door every night and slide into the back seat of a cab, looking so worn-out after her shift.

Would she even take a night off when he tried to insist on it?

Of course not. She claimed they were still staffed too thinly, and worked yet another night in a row. And if she was right, that didn't make it any easier to watch.

The fact that his heart hurt every time he looked at her was another problem. One that he kept to himself, although he felt his mother's gaze rest sadly on him from time to time, and knew she knew.

He'd watched Grace all through October, even as he kept his distance and tried to look at her as a younger sister or cousin. He'd seen the way she flinched sometimes at the sound of an unfamiliar voice, and didn't relax again until she searched out the voice's owner and reassured herself that it wasn't who-ever she feared.

The strength of his need to find that person, the man Grace feared in every unidentified voice, and beat him until he lay hurt and bleeding on the ground, came close to frightening Tyler.

A series of ringing, feminine laughs broke out at the far end of the bar, and he saw uncomfortably that all four women, including his innocent Grace, were staring at him with wickedly speculative looks in their eyes. Then they turned back to each other and laughter burst out again.

Tenderly patting his ego—after all, they couldn't be laughing *at* him, could they?—Tyler watched as Grace rang a total bill on the ladies' check and collected three credit cards without visibly flinching at the thought of splitting the bill three ways. After the women signed their tabs, Grace smiled at them and said something more in a low voice that had the women giggling again as they made their way out the front door, hopefully to return to bosses tolerant of long Friday lunches.

As Grace made her way back up the bar, a self-satisfied grin on her face, another wave of desire washed over him, making him want simply to tuck her under his arm and hang on to her forever. Instead he managed to comment lightly, "I see you worked your magic. How'd you do it?"

"Piece of cake, *darlin'*." She patted his butt casually as she squeezed past him. Tyler felt himself jump and cursed himself for a fool.

"Let me guess. They now think I have some bizarre medical condition?" At an even more disturbing thought, he narrowed his eyes and drilled a hole in the back of her neck as she ducked beneath the bar and crossed to the outside. "If you even mention the word impotent, I'll be over this bar with my hands around your neck so fast—"

"Relax, Romeo," she teased. The chat with the women seemed to have cheered her up. "Your Don Juan reputation is safe."

"So? Cough it up, Grace."

"Well, first off, I mentioned that they'd been coming in here fairly regularly, and then agreed with them when they said they couldn't think of a better way to spend lunch than looking at your ass." She grinned and hopped up on a bar stool. "Didn't you ever wonder why they were constantly asking you to pull different bottles from the beer coolers? Surely you didn't think they actually wanted to compare the labels."

"What are you saying? That they wanted to—"

"Watch you bend over?" Her grin could scarcely fit on her face. "You bet."

Tyler felt himself flushing. He was used to flirting, enjoyed it, and thought he was good at making a woman feel special, attractive. But this was something else. The thought that three women were calculatingly setting him tasks for the sole purpose of watching his butt was highly embarrassing.

"And I suppose when they accidentally dropped their money on the floor when they handed it across the bar to me, that wasn't really an accident."

Grace laughed hard enough to lose her breath and shook her head. "Not hardly."

Good Lord. He wanted to fan himself, his face was so hot.

"What did you say to make them stop all this?"

Her eyes widened. "Not a thing. You just told me to get rid of them." She clapped a hand over her mouth. It did nothing to hide her smile. "I'm afraid they'll be dropping dollar bills on the floor for a long time to come."

"Grace," he growled at her.

"Don't worry, they're just teasing, especially after I told them how great it was that they were such steady customers of the tavern. You know, since most restaurants run in the red for the first five years. And since you're undoubtedly going to be broke as a college student for the next couple of years, it's sweet of them to help you out." She fluttered her eyelashes at him. "They promised to come in at least three times a week for lunch, and they'll bring their friends."

Tyler needed to confirm what he was hearing. "Because they think I'm a charity case?"

"Do you care?" Grace shrugged at him. "They're nice ladies, but they *are* serious husband-hunters. This way, they'll still come here and spend money, but you're basically safe from the total come-on."

He just gaped at her, torn between gratitude and being offended.

Meanwhile, Grace had started tapping her fingernails sharply against the varnish of the bar. Her eyes locked on her rapidly moving fingers.

"Is that night off you mentioned still available?"

"What? Yes. Of course it is. Tomorrow will be crazy, but

take Sunday night off. Monday, too, if you want it. You've certainly put in enough hours in the last week, and you should have some regular days off anyway.''

''So should you, you know. You ought to think about a night off yourself.''

What was this sudden concern on her part? Grace looked edgy and still kept her head down. ''I might, at that. Spencer offered to watch the bar for me on Sunday night, since it should be quiet.''

As he watched, she twisted a cocktail straw until it was tied in knots. She stopped abruptly as if suddenly noticing what her hands were doing, and threw the straw in the trash with a grimace.

Her eyes, when she turned her face toward him, were not quite happy.

''Why don't you come over for dinner on Sunday, then?''

Six

"**W**hat on earth was I thinking?"

Grace demanded the question of her closet, standing in front of the open door for the sixth time on Sunday morning. She'd already raced through two loads of laundry and an hour at the ironing board in a desperate attempt to find something suitable to wear for dinner with Tyler. Crossed off the list were jeans and a T-shirt or shorts and a halter top, both too casual. Slacks and a blouse, too much like work clothes. The one short, cocktail dress she'd brought with her, God knows why, was much too dressy.

Even when she considered going out and buying something specifically for this evening, a thought that made her shudder, the idea of having an unlimited selection did not help. Apparently there was nothing on earth that made sense when you were cooking dinner for a man who was not only your boss but also someone who had told her he might be tumbling into caring about her.

But probably was not.

And what on earth was she doing cooking dinner for him, anyway?

Grace still wasn't quite sure exactly what had possessed her on Friday afternoon to invite Tyler over for a dinner that was now less than eight hours away. Temporary insanity, perhaps, inspired by the fun she had teasing him about being a sex object. Or by the odd possessiveness she felt lately toward him, tempting her to keep an extra glass of Cabernet on hand just in case she needed to conveniently spill it on the nearest over-aggressive flirter.

Regardless, she was now standing in front of a plundered closet, clothes strewn about the room, one forgettable blouse flapping like a windsock on the rotating fan, and it seemed increasingly likely that she would be cooking in the nude.

Deciding that the tornado-blast look of her bedroom was a cry for help if she ever saw one, Grace went to call in the Marines.

Sarah's bedroom door hung invitingly half open. Grace clutched the door frame and leaned into the room, letting a thread of panic leak into her voice.

"Help," she croaked. "Please help."

Sarah sat huddled on her bed, intently curled over a thick textbook, a pencil clenched between her teeth. Her eyes slowly focused on Grace. "Did you say something?"

"Help. No clothes. Making dinner for your brother. Must not be naked."

Sarah slammed the textbook closed with a resounding *whap* and promptly threw it across the room. She popped up off her bed like a cork shooting from a champagne bottle and raced over to clasp Grace's hand in her own. "Bless you. If I had to memorize the Latin name of one more intestinal parasite I might have thrown the towel in on veterinary medicine altogether."

"My pleasure. I am in dire need of fashion inspiration, or else I'm going to be standing over a stove in nothing but an apron." Grace looked at her watch. "In less than eight hours."

"Fortunately for you," Sarah announced as she flung her

closet door open with a flourish, "I adore dressing other people." She glanced down at her daily uniform of jeans and a T-shirt and then shrugged. "Not that you could tell by the way I dress myself."

Fifteen minutes later, after a quick buzz throughout the slim selection in Grace's own wardrobe, she was dressed. And dressed perfectly.

They stood in front of the bathroom's full-length mirror together. Sarah had talked Grace into the long straight column of a black jersey skirt and a spaghetti-strap tank top in ice-blue silk, combined with casual black sandals and a chunky silver necklace.

"See? Perfect," Sarah said as she finagled the clasp on the necklace. "The skirt's a little demure, the tank top a little sexy. Sandals to show you're not trying too hard, and the necklace because I like it."

"I may be crazy, but I look terrific." She hugged Sarah to her for a moment. So this is what it felt like to have a sister. "Thank you, Sarah."

Sarah surveyed her creation with pride. "I told you. I love dressing up other people." A quick tug on the skirt straightened its fall. "In fact, I still think you two should go someplace swanky, because that scarlet slipdress I've got would look incredible on you. And the poor thing is begging to be worn out on the town. I never have the time." She grimaced. "Or the date."

Grace heeded the frown and refrained from quizzing Sarah about her love life. Hoping to distract her, and to nip any misconceptions in the bud, Grace told her, "This is not a date. I'm just cooking dinner for Tyler because I can't afford a gift to say thank-you for taking me on, and because…" She struggled to come up with another reason. "Because the man needs someone to make him take a night off."

"Whatever you say, sister." Sarah stood behind Grace, pulled her shoulders back and pushed her chin up. "My work here is done. And intestinal parasites wait for no woman. Knock him dead."

All Grace could think, staring at herself in the mirror, was that if Tyler made fun of how she was dressed, she'd knock him on his ass.

The little voice in her head that she normally listened to, the voice that was sane and conservative and in charge of keeping her safe, was apparently locked in the cellar of her mind, not to be let out for the time being.

But Grace could hear it pounding on the door, warning her of danger ahead.

The only thing that let her remain calm, her safety net, was that she was cooking dinner for Tyler at Sarah's place.

I suppose I should think of it as *our* apartment. But the important thing is that even if Sarah isn't here, Tyler isn't likely to try some kind of grand seduction if his little sister can walk in the door at any moment. She'd realized that fact as the words inviting him over had tumbled from her lips. Tyler probably wouldn't be thinking of sex in his sister's apartment.

Or, better put, he wouldn't actually plan to *have* sex in his sister's apartment. There was no telling what the man might be thinking.

She, on the other hand, couldn't stop thinking about Tyler and sex and her room at all. Or to be more honest, *her* room, the bathroom, the kitchen table...

At three o'clock in the afternoon on a clear-sky Sunday in late October, blessedly warm with an Indian summer breeze, without a moment's warning, the safety net vanished.

"I'm so sorry, Grace," Sarah apologized, pacing the floor in the kitchen. She had just hung up the phone. "But Todd never calls me up and asks to come over. And he definitely never tells me that he 'wants to talk.'"

"Of course you have to see him. Don't worry, I understand."

"I just don't know if he's coming to break up with me or to ask me to marry him."

Grace tilted her head to the side and wrinkled her nose.

"I know it doesn't make any sense, but those are the only

two things I can think of that would make him do this. What I don't get is, why it has to be here."

"Well, don't make yourself crazy worrying about it." *I'll just make myself crazy wondering if I'll ever work up the nerve to do this again.*

"I know. But, Grace, your dinner plans are ruined. I feel like such a jerk." She dropped into a chair at the tiny kitchen table and cradled her head in her hands. Her voice was muffled by the long fall of her hair. "Todd is the jerk. The last-minute jerk."

Grace let out a breath and shrugged mentally. "It's okay. Really. The whole evening probably wasn't a good idea to begin with."

"Shut up. It was a great idea, and it would've been a great dinner if that sauce in the fridge I stuck a finger into was anything to go by." Sarah grinned out at her from between spread fingers, hiding her face. Then she jumped up out of the chair—"Wait a minute!"—and sprinted out of the room. Grace heard a drawer open and papers rattle, as if subject to a frantic search. "Aha!" And then Sarah was dancing back into the kitchen, a set of silver and gold keys on a ring dangling from her pointed finger.

"Guess who these belong to?"

Pushing a chair in front of her like a lion-tamer, Grace held her off.

"Absolutely not, Sarah. No way."

"Chicken. I'll even help you carry everything over there."

"No way," she repeated, frantic for a way out of this. "He won't have something, salt, pepper. Plates. It'll never work."

"Hey, my brother's a modern man. I bet he even has his own cheese grater." Sarah broke into a slow waltz around the kitchen with an imaginary partner, leering at Grace over her shoulder. "Besides, it'll be so much more private."

Exactly what I don't want.

"I am not cooking dinner for Tyler at his place. Impossible."

An hour later she watched as Tyler's apartment door closed

behind Sarah. She flipped the dead bolt closed reflexively and then stood frozen, staring at a featureless white door. After a moment, she rotated slowly on one heel, took a deep breath and walked slowly toward the kitchen.

Along the way, she trailed a hand along the back of a long, deep couch in the main room. A velvet nap, in navy, to balance out the feminine feel perhaps. The clack of her sandals on the hardwood floor disappeared in the thick pile of an Oriental rug blanketing the floor. A few pieces of wood furniture, with Shaker simplicity, were scattered around the room. In the same spare fashion, framed black-and-white photos decorated the plain white walls.

Feeling enough like a Peeping Tom already, she deliberately averted her eyes as she walked past Tyler's open bedroom door. Not, however, before she noticed an unmade bed and a pillow abandoned on the floor. Reassuring signs of mess in what was otherwise a terminally neat apartment.

Once in the kitchen, she discovered that Sarah was indeed correct. Tyler not only did possess his own cheese grater, but also a variety of pots and pans, colanders in *three* different sizes and every tool from a garlic press to a twenty-function food processor.

Undoubtedly, the man could cook.

What was already an attack of nerves threatened to mature into a full-blown panic.

Don't think. Just cook.

She peeled and then grated fresh ginger, shredding the tough lemony fibers against the rough steel perforations. Diced onions with her eyes clenched almost closed and hoped she wouldn't end up bleeding on the vegetables. Julienned carrots and cut up cauliflower into bite-size florets. Whisked tarragon-infused white-wine vinegar with a flurry of spices.

After half an hour of prep work, she decided that what she really needed was a glass of wine, so she uncorked the spicy Australian Shiraz she'd brought and poured herself one.

"Besides, the wine really ought to breathe." She toasted

herself and made sure the oven was preheating. Then she went to invade Tyler's CD collection.

Kansas City jazz was wailing brassily from the speakers and the scents of richly spiced dishes permeated the air when Tyler unlocked the door to his apartment and stepped into his fantasy.

He kicked off his shoes at the door and walked with silent, padded footsteps to the kitchen doorway. Pausing there, he watched Grace sway in place to the music, standing in front of the stove with a wooden spoon in one hand. The tips of her blond hair skimmed her shoulders, catching briefly on the skinny straps of her tank top. Ignoring the spoon, she dipped a finger into a pot for a sample.

"It smells delicious. How does it taste?"

She whirled around. Wide bright eyes and her finger still stuck in her mouth gave her the look of a startled five-year-old. She pulled the finger out, sucking on it reflexively. "Delicious. You know, if you scare the cook into a heart attack, dinner might arrive a little late at the table."

"Sorry." He walked over to where an open bottle of wine and an empty wineglass sat on the counter. "May I?" The garnet liquid flowed richly into the glass. "So, what are you concocting over there, mademoiselle chef? Or should I call you mem'sahib?"

"Let's put it this way. If you don't like Indian food, it's going to be a long, hungry night." She picked her own glass up off the counter and sipped it.

He stepped closer, deliberately crowding her, watching her back up a pace before deciding to hold her ground. With a slight movement, he clinked his glass delicately against hers.

"Fortunately, I happen to love Indian food. Anything spicy appeals to me."

Her mouth opened slightly, small teeth glistening wet behind bare lips. A moment passed. She pressed her lips firmly together and stepped around him to turn off a flame on the stovetop. "Good. Because it's just about done." She looked up at him and bit her lip. "I wasn't sure where we should eat. Your kitchen table is a little small for all the plates."

"We'll eat in the living room," he told her, and was immediately happy he'd bought the ridiculously tiny kitchen table Maxie had suggested. "You finish up in here and I'll set the table."

At least the cleaning lady came on Saturday mornings, he thought at the sight of his orderly living room. Then he began to set the scene.

In the kitchen, Grace let out a pent-up breath in a rush of air and sagged gently against the warm stove edge. Even after her heart had restarted itself from the shock of him suddenly there in the doorway, her nerve ends had refused to settle down. Sizzling beneath her skin until she swore she could feel the air move on her neck when he lifted his glass across the room.

Shake it off, Grace. Remember, this is just a friendly dinner. Don't panic.

Panic! Panic! the voice of caution locked in the cellar was shouting, lips pressed to a crack in the door. Grace ignored it.

She got to work, transferring the various dishes from pots and pans to bowls and platters, and then stepped back to survey her work. A baked, marinated, fall-off-the-bone chicken dish. *Dal,* a staple Indian food made from lentils, and basmati rice. Spicy corn and a tangy carrot and cauliflower pickle. Flat *nan* bread, and *raita,* the ever-present yogurt sauce in Indian meals, cool and refreshing.

Good grief. I've made enough food for an army.

"I may have gone a little overboard," she called to the other room and picked up four plates at once, in true waiter style. She strode into the living room. "But you can always eat it for lunch tomorrow. And dinner and—"

Only an instinct to keep the food on the plates stopped her from halting suddenly in shock.

Tyler's idea of setting the table for dinner and hers were polar opposites. At least for tonight. She'd assumed they would simply sit on the couch, preferably at opposite ends, and eat off the coffee table. A casual, friendly meal.

Well, casual still applied, but friendly seemed to have transformed itself into sensually romantic.

They would indeed be dining at the coffee table, but Tyler had dragged it into the middle of the Oriental rug and placed bed pillows on either side of it, so that two people sitting cross-legged on the floor would face each other across the table. The overhead lights were extinguished, and a half dozen white candles of various sizes clustered on either end of the table. Silver flatware and crystal glasses caught and threw off flickering light from the candles. The jazzy brass band duels had been replaced by Billie Holiday, crooning softly about her lover man.

"Well," she began and stopped. Tyler plucked the plates from her unfeeling hands and spread them on the coffee table, seemingly oblivious to her gape-faced shock. She tried again. "This is, um, awfully romantic, Tyler." He straightened and regarded her evenly. "Don't you think?"

"I thought your meal deserved something a little more special than paper plates on our knees." He wasn't teasing her, she could see. Just speaking honestly. "If you like, we can turn the lights on and the music off."

"No, no. Of course not." She felt foolish now. "This is lovely. I'll bring in the other dishes."

"No, you won't. You'll sit, pour yourself some more wine and relax. I can still bring out plates from a kitchen without dropping them."

Shoes seemed inappropriate, so she left them by the front door, lined up neatly next to Tyler's. At the table, she looked at the pillow on the floor and then her straight black skirt. Shrugging, she hiked the skirt up until its slit was high enough to allow her to drop gracefully into a cross-legged seat on the pillow. The scent of Tyler rose from beneath her, subtle and distracting with the thought that he had slept on the pillow on which she was now sitting. She squirmed in place for a second, uncomfortable with the idea.

Tyler's return to the room froze her in place. She could still smell him. She wondered if he slept naked.

Stop that, she scolded herself. There will be no picturing

Tyler naked. Put some food on your plate and think about something, anything else. Think about baseball.

"How about those Cubbies?" she asked Tyler as he sat across from her, and immediately grimaced at her own perky tone. Tyler looked at her as if confused by her sudden interest in Chicago's northside ball club. She wondered if he could tell that she was using baseball to keep herself from asking him if he slept in the nude.

Get hold of yourself, Grace. He's just a man, like any other you've dealt with.

Unfortunately she didn't buy that one, not for a second.

"I'm not holding my breath, but if we pray hard for a bull-pen, they've still got a shot at the post-season," Tyler answered her cautiously. Grace pasted an idiot's smile on her face and nodded, incapable of conversation at the moment. He spooned portions of each dish onto his plate and, picking up a round flat of *nan* bread, tore off a piece and built himself a mouthful, lamb, rice, *raita.* "Did you see Donnie the other night during the game?"

She nodded and relaxed. Talking about work was easy. And Donnie, a little old man with a bushy mustache and an Indiana Jones' fedora eternally on his head, had quickly become one of her favorite regulars. "In the ninth inning, when the bases were loaded with a three-two count? I thought he was going to have a heart attack." She lifted her own *nan*-wrapped morsel to her mouth and ate it neatly, giving a discreet lick to her fingers before brushing them on her napkin. Did she imagine Tyler's eyes narrowing a fraction of an inch and returning over and over again to her mouth?

"You should have seen him when I gave him his tab. Talk about heart attack." He smiled and shook his head. "I keep telling him that if he insists on buying drinks for the bar whenever the Cubs hit a homer, he's going to be a poor man. And I'll be a rich one. We may not have any pitching, but we can get the ball over the fence."

"Ah, so it's just business to you, hmm, tough guy?" she

teased him, finding herself somehow more relaxed than she'd felt in weeks.

"Exactly, just business."

"Then that wasn't you I saw taking twenty percent off his bill?" Tyler reached for the *raita* spoon. She reached out and pushed playfully at him, then gasped as she accidentally shoved his hand knuckles-deep into the yogurt sauce. He swore in surprise as she apologized, laughing, "Oops. Sorry about that."

"Witch. Look at this mess." He waved his dripping hand threateningly at her. Pointing a finger at her, he shook it, drips of sauce flying and spattering the table. "I ought to—"

She grabbed his hand and popped his finger into her mouth, licking at the cool, creamy sauce. The move was reflexive and shut him up instantly. His finger was hard and calloused in her mouth as she circled it with her tongue, pulling back slowly until her lips just kissed the tip. With a last flick of her tongue, she straightened and looked at him levelly.

His hand hung in the air above the table for a moment longer until he visibly shook himself and retracted it.

"If I'd known that was what it took," he muttered as he finished up the cleaning job himself, "I'd have rolled around in my dinner ages ago."

She laughed deep in her throat and took another sip of wine. Tyler watched her, rising desire warring with puzzlement on his face. Grace couldn't blame him. After so many weeks of tiptoeing around him on a daily basis, careful not to let herself think of him as anything more than her boss, her sensual attack had surprised her, too. But somewhere between the moment he'd sat and when he'd begun to scold her for the mess she'd made, a switch had flipped in her head, her body, her heart.

The heady, feminine power coursing now through her system was a new feeling for Grace, but one grounded in her certainty that he wanted her. And in her equal certainty, admitted fully for the first time, that she wanted him, too, and was through pretending that she wasn't going to give in to that desire. She'd made the decision yesterday, when she'd invited him to dinner, but hadn't allowed herself to acknowledge the reason.

Now she did, and the thought alone was thrilling. *I want Tyler, and tonight I am going to go to bed with him.* Everything else in her life was off balance and happening to her without her consent. This was one thing she owned, one area where she made the rules, because Tyler had promised not to push and she trusted him not to.

"Grace?"

"Relax, Tyler." The feeling of control was a powerful one, making it unnecessary to watch her words. Or to give in too soon to the temptation she fully intended to pursue. "Just pursuing a momentary impulse."

"Pursue away," he said, and leaned forward on his elbows to eye her with fascination. "Is there anything else you'd like to lick off me? And if so, please be specific about the body part."

She laughed and waved him off, gesturing at the still over-burdened table. "Just eat. We have enough food here for a small country."

"Or for breakfast." Testing.

When she just raised an eyebrow and then smiled at him, he fell over onto the floor, groaning theatrically.

"Have mercy, Grace. You're killing me."

"Better finish your last meal then. Wouldn't want you to die a hungry man." She took another bite of her food, felt a morsel catch at the side of her mouth and used the tip of her tongue to remove it. "Are you hungry, Tyler?" The boldness of her sexual teasing was intoxicating.

And intensely frustrating if you were on the receiving end, apparently. She delighted in the sight of Tyler pressing his pillow to his face and pretending not to hear her. After a moment, he sat up again.

"I'm going to pretend you're still my little, innocent Grace and eat my dinner," he said almost primly. His eyes moved loftily around the room, refusing to rest on hers. He spread *dal* on warm bread and chewed it absently, eyes focusing on her after a minute. "This is terrific, by the way. I'm very impressed that you know how to cook all of this from scratch."

"Mmm, hmm." Her mouth was conveniently full as she thought guiltily of the cookbook stuffed in her bag. She swallowed. "Sure you are."

"What's that supposed to mean?"

"I saw your kitchen, Tyler. I cooked in it for half the afternoon, for crying out loud." At his look of confusion, she flung up her hands. "You've got a million and one gadgets and devices. A spice rack that rivals a gourmet chef's, and an oven the size of my recent hotel room. You obviously cook like a whiz. I'm sure my managing to put a meal together doesn't impress you at all."

His slow smile was a mystery to her. "Aha. You obviously didn't open the upper right-hand cabinet by the sink."

"Why? What's in it?"

"Stacks of cookbooks. I don't mind cooking, but without a recipe, I'm pretty much limited to boiling water for pasta. But you're amazing, this meal is incredible."

The guilt was enough to have her breaking into giggles. When he looked at her curiously, she half leaned and half crawled her way past the end of the table to where her leather bag rested against the couch. Lifting the flap and loosening the drawstring, she tugged it open and flashed the contents at him. Perched smack on top was her one and only cookbook.

"Aha, a fellow connoisseur. You're still brilliant." He toasted her with chicken and basmati rice. "What else do you conjure up in your kitchen?"

"This is it," she said, and shrugged. "I bought this cookbook when I needed to make something for a dinner party, and I got so many compliments that I never bothered to get another one. All I know how to make is Indian food."

She tensed for a moment as she heard herself casually mention throwing a dinner party, as if that were something the average diner waitress did at the drop of a hat. In truth, she usually had her parties catered by one of the Haley restaurants. She searched frantically at bookstores that morning for the cookbook, an identical copy to the only one she owned. When it seemed that he didn't find anything wrong with her story, she relaxed again.

"You're a woman with fascinating talents, Grace. Who else knows what you've got hidden in there?" He laid his hand over hers on the table and curled his fingers around hers.

She changed the subject rapidly, feeling he was moving too close to topics that would require out-and-out lies on her part, something she was uncomfortable enough with having done already. Lying to him while sitting across the table and sharing a meal seemed unnecessarily hard and rude.

Tyler went along with the new conversation easily enough, and they spent the next hour comfortably talking about the restaurant, sharing ideas for possible improvements and concerns over where routines were still breaking down. Watching him talk about his business, Grace could see the shine that slid over him, the excitement that lit him up until she could practically see the light streaming from the tips of his fingers and shooting out the ends of his hair. He was filled with it, pure passion and vision and the steel-wrapped determination to make it all happen by sheer force of will if necessary.

Her hands itched to reach out and grab hold of him, to hang on until she managed to absorb some of that certainty and confidence into herself. That absolute conviction that what you were doing was the right thing, the only thing, possible in your life.

Tyler leaned back from the table, resting on his palms. Groaning, he pushed his plate in, away from the table edge, and let his eyes close slowly. "I think I should have stopped eating a half hour ago, but I just couldn't make myself."

"That's my favorite compliment," she said, and smiled. Half rising to her knees, she started stacking plates, putting his on top of hers.

"Stop." He didn't bother to open his eyes, but she halted anyway. "You cooked. You don't clean. I do." His head dropped even farther forward until his chin rested on his chest. "Tomorrow."

"All right." She settled back onto her pillow. In her wineglass, guttering candles flickered hypnotically, caught in the fragile curve of glass, dancing. The song rolling quietly from the speakers was instrumental, bass, piano, tapping cymbals, a wave of background noise like surf crashing on the shore at a beach house. Ever-present, unobtrusive, calm.

She sipped her wine and held it in her mouth, letting the earthy tannins swell and burst on her tongue before swallowing. When she inhaled, she breathed the scent of the wine and intoxicated herself in the quiet.

The clink of the glass's base hitting the coffee table was loud in the still room. Tyler looked up.

"This isn't working," he growled, and stood in one smooth movement. Striding in two steps around the table to where she sat, he dropped abruptly to the floor at her side. Grace tensed. This was what she wanted, but she wasn't sure she was ready for it. Despite all her bravado, her sexual past was limited to a few fumbling, lukewarm encounters that had left her feeling untouched. Now her insides were trembling with nerves and she wished Tyler had waited for her to make some kind of move. She'd wanted that illusion of control so badly.

Tyler stretched his legs and body out on the floor, rolled onto his side, and put his head in her lap.

"Ah." Contentment colored the sigh. "Perfect."

Grace looked down at the man whose head rested gently in her lap, his eyes closed, the lids shadowed a purple the color of bruises, a visible symbol of the hours he gladly worked for his passion. As she watched, his breath slowed and deepened. He moved once, pulling one leg up to rest his knee on the floor at his side, and wedging a hand between his head and her thigh. But then he lay still, quietly sleeping, and she felt a peaceful calm creep over her. After a few minutes she began softly stroking his hair, running her fingers gently through the strands, down the line of his neck and across his shoulders. Comforting him, she supposed, although she didn't know why she felt that he needed it.

Another candle burned out and the light dimmed further. The music drifted further into the background and time slowed until each moment lasted an eternity. The sensation was so unfamiliar that it tugged at her. Grace realized that for weeks she'd been running, constantly moving or hustling, for a job, a solution, a tip from table three. She hadn't had time to simply sit still and breathe.

In the quiet room she sat and she breathed. A centering calm unfolded in her like a flower and spread balancing petals wide through her body, grounding her. She looked at Tyler and felt a surging wave of gratitude for the sanctuary he'd provided her, and the space he'd allowed her that had, in turn, let her give him this night of rest. Tenderness bloomed with warmth in her hands and she brushed them softly over his curled arm.

When her back began to ache and her eyelids grew more than a little heavy themselves, she stirred. Cradling Tyler's head, she managed to snag his pillow and drag it beneath the table to exchange her thigh for it as a headrest. His sleep was deep enough that he simply rolled over to curl up on his other side, facing her. Grace could see her shoes lined up neatly at the door, her leather bag propped up at the end of the couch, and knew she should leave.

The decision to curl up next to Tyler on the thick pile of the Oriental rug was instinctive and undeniable. Without thought, she rested her head on the same pillow and settled comfortably on her side. She'd thought to control this evening, to take charge of a flirtation that would lead with a magnetic pull to something sexual, a release to the tension she carried around in her body like armor. Instead, the tension had seeped out of her so slowly that she hadn't noticed, until she found herself here, boneless in relaxation on the floor next to this man whose kindness and humor and desire were tugging her inevitably closer to him.

The warmth of another body next to his triggered an instinct in Tyler that had him curling an arm around her and tucking it under her side. He pulled her close, until his knees were tucked behind hers, her butt pressed against his groin. She was enfolded and, held so securely, dropped almost immediately into sleep.

When she woke, it was to darkness and silence. Darkness and silence and a low voice, from a man who'd noticed her sudden alertness, whispering in her ear.

"Please tell me this is Grace I've got curled up with me, so nice and warm. Because otherwise, I've been fantasizing about waking up the wrong woman."

Seven

___

Grace took a deep breath. And realized that the hand previously wrapping her waist was now cupped around her breast, a thumb rubbing almost idly across the hardening peak. She hadn't been able to wear a bra with the tank top, and the sensation of silk pulling gently across her nipple was exquisitely isolated in the still quiet dark.

A quiet that was broken by the sudden, uncontrollable sound that escaped her as Tyler's fingers curved and feathered lightly against the side of her breast. His breath moved the hair on her neck. Her voice broke audibly on a sigh.

"Grace?" A question.

"Yes." The answer to anything he was asking of her. His voice murmured again, questioning further, but she interrupted, "Shh, yes." A repeated whisper. "Yes."

Moonlight slid through the window, highlighting the edge of skin, a faint sheen of light on curves and flat planes. Her bare arm. The broken arch of his fingers wrapped around her. He pulled away, pressed against her shoulder to lay her back flat against the carpet. The dark shadow of him leaned above her, blocking out the moonlight, his mouth and eyes darker magnets. In the dark, there was feeling only to tell her that he dipped his head, one arm curved at the top of the pillow, fingers tangling in her hair. The other resting motionless on her hip.

The heat of his mouth held, hovering, just above her breast, radiated against her skin. An eternity, waiting, until she arched her back to press her breast against his mouth. Her shoulders scraped against the carpet, sharp rasping contrasting with the sudden damp heat of his mouth wetting silk and pulling gently at her nipple. She heard her own voice, soft breaking sounds in the stillness.

His hand moved at her waist, fumbling in the dark for the hem of her tank top and then sliding beneath it to skate his fingers across her stomach at the edge of her skirt. She opened her mouth on a gasp and he was there, plunging with sudden intensity into the kiss, his tongue tangling with hers, and she wrapped her arms around him to pull him deeper into her. Behind her closed eyelids, flowers of light burst and faded and were reborn in glowing colors on her inner vision.

By the time he pulled away, they were both breathing hard. His leg was wedged between hers and she could feel herself rocking instinctively against him.

"You—" a hand skated up her bare side "—have entirely too many clothes on."

In response, she let her arms fall from his shoulders to the floor over her head, crossed at the wrist. She turned her head toward him, hoping he could read the permission she gave in the arc of her body.

He saw, and seeing, bent over her again, repeating her name in barely audible murmurs against her skin.

His hands pushed the fabric of her shirt up, stopping, when it bunched at her shoulders, to suck and tease, flicking his tongue against her breasts by turns, covering her with hard hands that molded her breasts to guiding the peaks to his mouth. He slid the shirt higher, over her head and up her arms until it tangled at her wrists, where he held it in place with one hand and paused to look at her laid out in front of him.

She felt his gaze on her skin and opened her own eyes. Adjusted to the dark, she could still only make out the faintest outline of her body, a slightly brighter shine where the wetness of his mouth had touched her. His body was motionless against hers as he watched her. Lifting a hand, he ran a fingertip down the side of her face, barely touching her as he skimmed past her neck, her collarbone, across the rise of her breast. Over the sensitive tip and across her rib cage, to fall softly off at her side.

"You are so beautiful." He pressed a reverent kiss to the flat hollow between her breasts. "So perfect."

"No." She knew too well what she was, and that he did not know, and closed her eyes against the intrusions of the outside world. She wouldn't let it come here, between them, but she couldn't bear to let him say such things, when only she knew the truth. She whispered, "Not perfect. But here, now."

"And perfect," he said, and silenced her with his mouth, her hands still held above her.

His hand was hot, rising up the slit in her skirt, curling around her thigh to brush gently against her heat, sparking sharp, almost painful need. She barely noticed when he hooked his fingers in the skirt's elastic waistband and pulled, dragging her underwear down her thighs in the same movement. He bent her knees, pulled her legs toward him and tugged her clothes off over her feet without letting her arms up. Skirt and underclothes were tossed carelessly to the side.

The sudden exposure, as he trapped one of her knees beneath his while he lay at her side and used his free hand to push the other open wide, startled her into sudden awareness. Tyler was still fully dressed at her side. The hard seams of his jeans pressed into the knee he held against the floor. His T-shirt didn't conceal the heat radiating off his body where it pressed against the length of hers, hip, rib cage, arm, arching now in a reflexive instinct to cover herself.

"Lie still." His fingers slid achingly slow, up and down the sensitive skin of her thigh. "Just let me touch you."

His fingers skated across her stomach, connecting the ridges of her hipbones, before moving down her other thigh. Circling slowly around her lower body, spiraling in gradually, until hard cramps of desire seized her. Then he was skimming against her most sensitive flesh, barest touches that brushed again and again over her, through the wetness of her, tormenting. The building pressure was unbearable. She arched her head back. A weak voice cried, "Please, please," over and over again in the silence. And still he barely touched her. Unbearable. She thrust her hips up and pushed against his hand forcefully and the first crush of orgasm broke her apart in shards of colored light that shattered in front of her eyes.

She fell back, breathing hard with the sudden release, her body melting into the floor limply, hands freed from their temporary prison. In a moment, though, the world spun as Tyler pulled her to him and rolled over until he was flat on his back on the floor and she braced herself above him, hands pressed flat on his chest. A hand tangled in the hair at the nape of her neck brought her in close for an openmouthed kiss that swept the lethargy out of her veins in a rush.

Sensations rushed over her from all sides, her body warring with itself to feel everything at once. The suction of his mouth against hers. The scrape of a tongue drawing wetly. Fingertips dancing slowly down her spine to the top of her butt. A hand curving around her hip to pull the heat of her closer. The hardness of him pushing heavily against her thigh through his jeans.

Suddenly it was as important to touch him, to feel his skin beneath hers, as it was to revel in being touched by him, and her hands raced over his body with greedy searching. She tugged and pulled, and in a minute had him as naked as she was. The sheer pleasure of his skin against hers, the warmth and softness and intimacy of it was mind-fogging. She tangled arms and legs and body with his, until to move in any direction felt like a separation from him. And still her hands sped over him.

Everywhere, his muscles were hard, tensed until they almost shook, and she realized that he was holding himself in check, letting her decide what came next. He touched her, but he didn't rush or insist, waiting instead to see what she chose to do to him.

She sculpted out the feel of him with her hands, dragging them exquisitely slowly over the planes of his chest, the flexed muscles of his shoulders and biceps. His breathing caught, steadied, and caught again as she painted his body with open-mouthed kisses. The skin over his hard stomach was baby-soft, suddenly stretched tight with a gasp as her hand dipped lower and wrapped around him. He strained against her with a cry as she felt him shudder.

It was his turn to beg.

"Ah, Grace." His voice was strained in the night room. "Please." A sudden hiss. "I need—"

"I know," she whispered, a finger pressed to his lips. He took it into his mouth and sucked fiercely. She slid her body up his and raised herself over him again.

His fingers pressed into her hips, steadying her above him as she eased herself down, slowly taking him inside her. She pressed herself against him until she could get no closer, and then stopped, motionless, focused, absorbed in the feel of him stretching her body wide. His hands reached up through the darkness to cradle her face gently. For a long moment he held her and she wondered if he could see her in the dark, watching him, overwhelmed with feeling for him. With the feeling of him.

And then the pressure began to build again and she lost coherent thought. Her body of its own will began to rock slowly against him, and then faster, moving instinctively in a mindless search for her own pleasure.

She felt, through the haze, when Tyler reached a hand between them to brush lightly against her where her body joined slickly with his. Heat exploded and the sudden lightning crack of ecstasy jerked a harsh cry out of her.

Once, twice, he thrust against her with his hips, her own still moving rhythmically on sheer momentum. His guttural cry tore through her and she felt his muscles spasm beneath her. His hands clenched her hips and pulled her hard against him, before falling limply at his sides. Her body's movements slowed, until she fell forward against his sweaty chest, her hair damp at her neck and against her face.

His chest rose and fell raggedly under hers, and he wrapped his arms tightly around her, hugging her to him. Their breathing and the rush of her heartbeat in her ears were the only sounds in the silence.

He rolled her onto her side, legs tangled together, bodies still joined, and brushed the tangle of hair off her face. Then he pressed his hand briefly against the center of her chest, before repeating the gesture on himself.

"Just checking." At her wordless sound of query, "Making sure we're not dead."

She shook with silent laughter against him. Speech hadn't quite returned, but she was most definitely not dead. In fact, Grace couldn't remember ever feeling this alive. Every inch of her skin was aware, sensitive to the cooling feel of sweat drying in the cool air, the warmth of his body touching hers, the lingering tension where his body filled hers. She shivered.

"Cold?" He pulled away slightly from her.

"No, not—ah." Her breath hissed out, the aftershocks of their loving pulsing softly through her as he eased himself out of her. She felt him slide slowly from her body, leaving her feeling strangely hollow and empty. "Not cold. Just shivery."

"Shivery is good," he whispered, and kissed her face softly. "Shivery is very good."

She sighed and kissed him in return, trying to tell him without words how happy she was to be curled up with him on an Oriental rug in the middle of a dark living room, remnants of a meal scattered on a table next to them. Already she could feel the press of outside, daylight problems pushing at her thoughts and the rising tide of guilt and confusion threatened to break in on this moment. A moment where she could fool herself into believing that their world was as he'd seen her. Perfect.

"You know what I could do now?" Tyler whispered the words against her neck and bit her gently there.

"What's that?" She curved an arm around his neck, more than willing to be drawn away from her thoughts and back to the physical.

"Eat."

She yelped as his hand smacked her butt lightly. He rolled to his feet and stood in one motion, dumping her abruptly on the floor. She propped her head on one hand and glared up at him, knowing he couldn't see her face.

"For some reason—" she didn't need light to hear the laughter in his voice "—I am absolutely starving."

Her decision was already made. She braced herself in preparation.

"Race you to the kitchen." And ran.

Smacking her hand on the refrigerator handle, Grace claimed her victory. She tugged the door open a crack and then shrieked. The spill of bright light into the dark room was startling, as was the realization that she was standing buck-naked in the middle of Tyler's kitchen. In front of a window that looked out onto the street.

A window with no shade or curtain.

She sprinted past Tyler to the shelter of the doorway and stood there, laughing at herself.

"I take it back. You win." She heard him snort. "Winner brings plates back to the living room."

"Sounds like the loser's job to me," he complained, but she heard him rattling the lids off pots in the fridge.

In the living room, she snagged his T-shirt off the floor and pulled it on. It covered her butt, and that was about all. She shrugged and sank to the floor, wrapping her arms around her knees. She certainly wasn't trying to hide her nakedness from Tyler. Just any neighbors who happened to look in the window.

He returned with plates piled high and she dove on the food, suddenly ravenous herself. They fed each other and ate off their own plates, licked each other's fingers clean and kissed between bites of their late-night feast.

By meal's end, they were kissing more than they were eating and Grace's only fear was that they would forget the plates of leftover scraps at their sides. Visions of her and Tyler rolling around in their dinners, as he'd suggested he would do earlier, made her smile.

Sitting next to her, Tyler paused between nibbling on her neck and shoulder to ask, "Ready for one more race?"

"Oh?" She put one hand on the floor beside her, ready to push off. "Where to?"

She knew the answer to her own question.

"Bed." As expected.

What she didn't expect was that Tyler, instead of streaking past her, would catch her up along the way and haul her over his shoulder, where she bounced roughly all the way to the bedroom.

"Wait—oof! Tyler—ow!" She shrieked loudly enough to draw the attention of any neighbors not already attracted by the sight of her naked in the kitchen.

He dumped her unceremoniously on the bed and threw himself down next to her, bouncing them both on the mattress. She laughed and then groaned and clutched her stomach.

"You may have done—ow—permanent damage, Tyler."

"I couldn't resist." He rolled her over and tickled her with stiff fingers beneath her arms and at her sides, as she shouted and squirmed and wrestled to break free. "It's so much fun, making you shriek."

With a heave of her hips and a carefully placed shove, she threw him on his back and pinned him. "I'll show you shrieking." And did, as he reared up suddenly and nipped at her breast.

Before she could blink, their positions were reversed and it was Tyler who rose above her. He spoke in his best evil-villain voice. "Yes, you will."

By the time he worked his way down her body with his

mouth, his fingers had slipped from tickling to stroking, and her shrieks slid into shuddering moans.

Then he slipped inside her and she was wrapped in him, around him, and the night shattered again in front of her eyes.

She woke him once more in the night, already slipping over him as he rose to consciousness. They made love silently, slowly, and when she fell asleep again, it was with him still inside her.

He woke her in return when the alarm went off loudly before he smacked the snooze button. He pulled her beneath him, finally able to see clearly in the morning light. "It's set for a half hour early," he told her, and took her mouth.

She fell asleep again in a tangle of warm sheets, the sound of his shower faint in her ears.

She was vaguely aware of sounds, later, that might be someone pulling clothes from drawers and tugging them on. And the clatter of metal and porcelain tugged at her brain, their meaning not quite apparent.

But the smell of coffee was clear enough, even to her sleep-befuddled head, so she pulled on Tyler's T-shirt again and followed the scent into the kitchen. Tyler was sitting at the miniscule kitchen table, a mug of coffee at his elbow.

A second mug rested near the edge of the table closest to the door. Behind it was a small electric fan, pointing steadily toward the bedroom and blowing the scent of dark roast through the room.

"Cute." She grabbed the mug and turned to climb onto his lap, straddling him on the chair. Draping herself bonelessly against him, she brought her hands together behind his head and lifted the mug to her mouth, careful not to spill. She sighed. "Mmm, coffee. Good."

"Good morning to you, too, darlin'." His words were muffled in the fabric covering her shoulder. He pressed a kiss there. "Sleepy?"

"Waking up." She took another large swallow and felt the caffeine work its magic on her fuzzy head. "Are you leaving?"

"Duty calls. Or, at least, beer vendors do. And you have Sarah's spare key, so you can sleep as late as you like." He ran his hands up her bare thighs. "I wish I could stay here with you."

"Mmm." Her head was clearing, and with that, and more coffee, came interesting ideas. She dropped the mug on the table and pulled herself up straight. Her arms were draped over his shoulders, and she scraped her nails through the short hair at the back of his neck. "You could stay here." She pressed her mouth to his, teasing it open with her tongue. "Just for a little bit longer."

She felt him harden against her thigh and smiled with pleasure. Tyler's hands reached up to tug hers from his neck and hold them sedately at her sides. "Grace, I can't be late." He still held her hands, so she brushed her breasts against him and felt him flinch. Eyes with heavy lids locked with his, she pressed herself against his lap and made herself tremble. "Grace. I have people." A shudder. "People waiting. I can't be late."

With a quick tug, she was free and snaking her hands down to his waist, working swiftly at his jeans. When he sprang free into her hands, she held him strongly.

"If you can't be late," she told him, feeling wicked and loving it, "then you'll just have to be fast."

She took him into her and felt the light breaking through her again.

When she woke again, the light was shining intensely through the window and the apartment was silent around her. She slid out of bed, still in Tyler's T-shirt, and walked to the bathroom, wincing slightly at the soreness in her thighs and other, more intimate places. The thought made her smile.

In the bathroom, she caught herself in the mirror and the smile faded. Her blond hair was knotted from hours of passion and sweat. Nonetheless, her roots showed clearly the chestnut hair growing in and this obvious sign of her deception was enough to stop her cold.

She leaned over the sink, unhappy with the picture reflected opposite her. The woman in the mirror looked well-loved, lips swollen and red from rough kisses. A faint bruise was emerging on her thigh where Tyler had gripped her hard in the previous night's dark. The shadows under her eyes spoke of a night not spent asleep.

She looked like a woman who'd spent the night making love.

Making love. The words rolled ominously around in her head. Making love. Not "having sex." Grace knew the difference, and knew what she and Tyler had done wasn't just sex. She'd known she was falling in love with him as she'd lain down to sleep with him on the floor last night; she'd chosen to stay anyway. She'd lain with him and been wrapped in his life as surely as she'd been wrapped in his arms. She couldn't argue with that.

Can't argue with it? The voice in her head was outraged. And bitter. *How real is it, Grace, when you say you're in love with the man and you don't trust him enough to tell him a goddamn bit of truth about yourself? How real is it, when everything he knows about you is a lie?*

"I *have* told him the truth, basically," she argued with herself in the mirror. She couldn't meet her own eyes. "He knows everything important about me."

Stop fooling yourself, damn it. You don't think the fact that you're Grace Haley, millionaire and restaurant powerhouse, is going to be considered an important thing? That your engagement to another man has been announced publicly in the society pages of several newspapers?

Get real.

In the shower, she pressed her face into the spray and let the water run over her face, her mouth open beneath the fall. She braced herself against the wall with her hands and leaned into the blast, scalding hot water coursing down her skin. The spray pounded at the top of her skull, but couldn't wash away the one thought that kept returning to her over and over.

She stepped out of the shower and wrapped a plush towel around herself, avoiding even a glimpse of herself in the fogged mirror. But she couldn't avoid the inescapable conclusion pushing to be acknowledged.

She made it to the bedroom, shutting out that voice. But the sight of the twist of sheets on Tyler's bed where she'd so recently slept with him was a smack in the face. She sank onto the edge of the mattress and dropped her head.

"Ah, damn." The pain was physical, a jagged tear chasing her heart beneath her breastbone.

She was a coward.

From the moment she'd left her restaurants, left her condo, her life, she'd been running. Running hard and fast enough to keep her own thoughts confused. Telling herself that she just needed the distance, the space to figure out what to do.

Instead of sticking to what she knew was right, she'd let other people intimidate and threaten her into giving up and fleeing the field. She'd yielded at the first push, to people who had no real power to hurt her, or her business.

Her mother certainly couldn't hurt her. She rarely bothered to stop in Chicago, in between her jaunts to the various tropical playgrounds of the wealthy and bored. An occasional request for more money to be deposited in her account was the extent of Grace's contact with her.

Not even her Charles, the titular head of her family's corporation, could cause her any real trouble. To begin with, his complete ignorance of the business limited his options to act. And with fifty percent of the company stock in her name, although Grace didn't hold a majority and couldn't get rid of him without support from other family members, support that would not be forthcoming, neither could he make any serious business decisions without her approval.

At least, he couldn't if she were there to state her refusal to go along with his commands.

"Damn it, what were you thinking?" Her fists were hard against her temples. She felt as though she'd pulled herself free of a pool of thick mud and was only now managing to clear the filth from her eyes. The foolishness of her actions was glaringly apparent to her, as it would be to anyone who was thinking straight.

Running away hadn't been the answer.

She knew the answer to make now, and that was to return to her life and fix her own problems.

To stop lying to the people she'd met here, people she was coming to care about.

The immediate release of the tension she'd been carrying around in her muscles for weeks on end was bodily sensation. Like having treated herself to a full massage. The relief was overwhelming, and a clear sign that she was making the right decision.

I don't know what happened to me. But somehow, after Grandmother died, I lost my way. I let Charles and Mother take control of my life. Somehow things got to the point so that when they *decided that Charles and I should get married, I didn't even have the strength of will to tell them no.*

But no more. I'll straighten out my business and my life, and settle matters with my family, and then I'll sit down with Tyler and explain to him who I am and why I lied to him about everything.

He would be mad. No doubt about that. In fact, perhaps mad was not the word. Irate. Furious. Angry beyond all attempts to repair. But she would make him listen. Hadn't he known from the beginning that she was holding back something from him? And hadn't he given her permission to do so, until year's end, as long as she came clean then?

You'd have until the end of the year to straighten out whatever problems you have, and I'll help you out any way I can. But on December thirty-first, New Year's Eve, you sign on one hundred percent, and there'll be no more hiding for you. Do we have a deal?

"You're damn right we do," she muttered as she pulled her clothes on. "We have a deal, and I'll even beat my deadline. Just give me a few more weeks to clear things up, and I'll come clean in before Thanksgiving, buddy, not December thirty-first."

As she gathered her things and then scraped the remaining dirty plates and started the dishwasher running, Grace was aware of that other, more cautious, voice in her head. And she listened, because it was making sense.

The best thing she could do, right now, would be to go find Tyler and tell him the truth about everything. Today. Immediately.

Because the *worst* thing that could happen right now would be for Tyler to find out the truth about her from someone else. Anyone else. If Grace could explain herself to Tyler, one on one, she just *might* be able to make him listen long enough to understand why she'd done all this. Lied to him about her name and history. Lied to his family. Run away from her own family and job. Let him think she was hiding from an abusive boyfriend and not a wealthy fiancé. And Tyler might possibly believe and understand her.

But only, let me repeat only, if you are the one to tell him, Grace. If he finds out from anyone else, well, can we say "fat chance"?

Tell him today.

The telephone handset was at her ear and she'd punched in most of the digits needed to call up Tyler at the bar when another truth of the situation occurred to her. She paused for a moment and then placed the handset back on its base.

The last thought to run through her head before she picked up the phone was how happy she was to be able to tell Tyler the truth, and how grateful she would be for the help and support he'd be sure to provide her in dealing with this mess of her family and business. She knew she would be able to rely on him completely, and that was a relief.

And then came the thought that stopped her cold.

Of course she would be able to rely on Tyler. That's what he did. He helped people in need, particularly women, even if he wasn't asked to do so. If she went to him now and told him about her slew of problems, he would be mad, yes, but his innate compassion would soon take over. He would jump at the chance to take care of her, at that point, and would start seeing her as someone who needed his protection. Tyler would help her patch up her life, and by the time he'd saved her, would probably decide he was in love with her. The relationship between them was already heading in that direction.

Grace remembered when she'd first questioned whether Tyler's feelings for her might be based on the protectiveness that sprang up naturally in him at the sight of a young woman, obviously on the outs, living in dangerous circumstances, looking for work and on the run from a bad relationship.

Wouldn't this simply be more of the same uncertainty?

If she went to Tyler, problems in hand, she would always be afraid that his feelings for her were based on concern and compassion, not love. And, although it had taken her a while to get here, Grace finally knew that she didn't want to be protected. Or loved because she needed protection.

She needed to be able to come to Tyler as her own person, needing nothing from him, but *wanting* so much more. She needed Tyler to love her for who she was, a woman in her own right, with her own life, and not a set of problems that needed him to solve them.

A quick run-through of her plan convinced Grace. All she needed was time. Just a few weeks, maybe less, and she would be able to go to Tyler as an adult, a woman asking for his understanding and his love, not his help.

It was risky. Grace acknowledged that. The safest course would be to confess everything now and make her own peace later with the uncertainty she felt regarding Tyler's affection.

But I've been playing it safe for most of my life. The first risky thing I ever did was to try to talk my way into an under-the-table job at Tyler's. And that's turned out pretty well so far. So if it comes down to taking a chance, in order to do what's right both for myself and for my relationship with Tyler, then I guess I'm up for that chance.

Decision made, Grace picked up the phone again, this time to call Paul. She needed one last favor from her close friend, and then she'd do her best to make sure he never had to worry about the future of his kitchen again. What she wanted him to do was easy enough to explain.

"Yes, *chérie,* your idiot fiancé still comes here, to his so-called 'office' every day. He pretend to be making phone calls and such, but mostly he sticks his dirty little fingers into my pots until I throw the knife at him."

"I need another favor, Paul."

"Anything, especially if it will get that peacock-head out of my kitchen."

Her next call was to her attorney. Grace hadn't contacted him since the day she'd left everything behind, other than to send him a note explaining specifically that she was taking a brief hiatus to mourn her grandmother and that she would be contacting him in a reasonable amount of time.

Perhaps most people would not consider several months to be reasonable, but the word was vague enough to make it impossible for anyone to act in her stead.

"Hello, Franklin. It's Grace Haley."

Somewhat to her surprise, Franklin did not sound particularly enthused to hear from her after such a long time. Perhaps he was understandably frustrated over the position in which she'd placed him. She was sure her family had tried to intimidate him into acting as her representative, knowing he possessed the authority to make a wide range of independent business decisions on Grace's behalf.

She got right to the point and explained what she planned to do.

"A gentleman named Paul Montcrasse will be calling you with the list of people to be contacted. You should hear from him this afternoon. Please arrange for those people to meet with me, as soon as possible, although I understand that many of them will need to travel quite a distance to get here."

"But, Ms. Haley, that could take weeks. And your fiancé—"

Boy, was she getting sick of that word.

"Make it clear that I expect them, or their representatives, immediately. We will use the penthouse suite at the Drake Hotel. In fact, put them all up at the Drake, Franklin, as a gesture of my appreciation for their trouble. I'll pay the bill personally.''

"But, Ms. Haley, I know that Mr. Huntington would want to meet with you before you make any rash decisions." Franklin's voice cracked with his agitation.

"Good God, Franklin. Anyone would think you were Charles's attorney, not mine." She couldn't prevent the irritation from rising in her voice. She tried to squelch it and was mostly successful. "Just set it all up please, and don't worry about Mr. Huntington. He will be taken care of, have no fear."

Eight

Pressing ice wrapped in a rough towel to the corner of her battered and bleeding temple, Grace decided that her official story for the bruised face was going to involve a car door, or perhaps an inauspiciously placed lamp. Anything but the truth.

That she'd been clocked in the head by a cell phone-wielding attorney was rather embarrassing.

That she'd very nearly been beaten up in a bar brawl that ended with a very small, but clearly annoyed, Chihuahua peeing on her, was simply humiliating.

She was definitely going with the car door story.

Pulling the towel away from her head for a moment, she grimaced at the sight of blood smeared on the cloth. Lovely. No doubt the bruised-and-bloodied look would go over well at the meeting she'd set up tomorrow at the Drake Hotel. She would be the picture of an accomplished and in control executive. Ha.

She wasn't even going to try to kid herself that makeup would be able to cover this.

And the week had started so promisingly.

She'd made full use of her second day off, taking Monday afternoon to touch up her roots and to hit the shops on Oak Street in search of a designer suit to spend every last penny of her savings from waiting tables on. It might be superficial, but Grace was fully aware of how much easier it was to command respect in a roomful of business people when you were wearing a fifteen-hundred-dollar Chanel suit. She considered the money well spent on her armor.

When she caught herself sneaking up the stairs of their apartment and praying that Sarah wasn't home, to notice and wonder at the suit bag emblazoned with the world-famous interlocking Cs, Grace decided that she would be very happy when her days of pretending to be someone else were over. The tension, and fear of getting caught in all her skullduggery, was weighing more and more heavily on her nerves as the clock ticked down to her day of resolution.

She reminded herself to find out if Sarah would be out of the house on the day of her meeting with the would-be restaurant buyers. Otherwise, she would have to rent yet another room at the Drake for herself, so she could dress in private, which verged on the ridiculous.

Using her condo as a base of operations for the day would solve many of her problems, but she didn't feel quite ready to go home yet. And she was certain that the minute she set foot in the front door, someone on staff would be calling Charles to alert him to her return. No doubt he paid well for that sort of information.

No, she would stay in hiding for just a little bit longer.

Monday evening, she had paced around the apartment, wondering if she should have stopped by the restaurant to see Tyler, and then thinking that she shouldn't assume they would be spending every night together from now on. A minute later she was scooping Ben & Jerry's Chunky Monkey ice cream out of a carton with a spoon, standing in front of the open freezer door, convinced that the previous night was definitely a one-time thing that Tyler probably didn't care about repeating.

When the phone rang and she'd shrieked, startled by the sudden noise, Grace had decided that her nerves might be the teensiest bit shot. She'd yanked the receiver off its base.

"Hello?"

"Why aren't you at my house?" Tyler's voice had been a low rumble in her ear.

She'd smiled and felt the heat of her own blush. "I didn't want to assume—"

"What? That I wouldn't want to come home at three in the morning and find you sleeping in my bed?" The words were a smooth caress. "Darlin', you can assume I'd like that every night of the week."

"All right, then." She'd set out to tease. "I hope you don't mind that I prefer to sleep in the nude."

He'd groaned. "You're trying to torture me, aren't you?"

"Is it working?"

"Just get your butt over to my place, will you? You've got the spare key." She had heard his grin over the wire. "I'm not quite up to crawling into bed with you when my little sister is sleeping down the hall, but I'll do it if you make me."

"I won't. Close up quickly. Darlin'."

"I'll try to get there as early as I can, but—"

"Don't be ridiculous. I know what it's like, remember? You'll get here when you can."

She could almost hear his surprise over the telephone. He'd thanked her and hung up and she'd known that someone in the past hadn't understood his willingness to devote himself to his work. She'd felt sorry for the woman who'd missed out on this man.

Not that she'd give him up if someone came knocking.

Since that evening a week ago, she had slept at Tyler's apartment almost every night, coming home with him after closing up the restaurant, making love before falling asleep in a tangle of arms and legs and breath.

One day she arrived at work to find out that Tyler's growing staff had been increased by the addition of Jack, a skinny but undeniably good-looking young man, who quickly picked up the routine. He turned out to be a whiz at charming ladies, particularly those who were old enough to be his mother. But after the fourth time he showed up more than an hour late for his shift, she decided to sit down with Tyler.

"It's not that I don't like him. When he's here, he definitely works hard, but…"

"But?"

"*When* he's here," she admitted. "I just don't think being here on time, or at all, is a big concern for him. He told me today that he was late because the girl he picked up last night wanted one last, uh, session."

"Really?" She suspected Tyler's mouth was twitching from amusement, not irritation.

"Yes, really. He told me that he's too young to turn down sex." At this, Tyler laughed out loud. Grace fumed. "I told him that when you're older, you learn how to set the alarm clock early enough to fit in sex *and* getting to work on time. His job should be important enough to him for that."

"I agree. So, that does it," he said, wringing out a bar towel over the sink.

"Whoa, wait a minute! I wasn't trying to get the kid fired." She should learn to keep her mouth shut. Tyler looked at her oddly.

"You didn't. And you can't," he said after a moment's pause. "Although I'm surprised you don't want to, since he's just making your job more difficult. But only Jack can get himself fired, which will happen if he comes in late again after getting a warning."

"Okay," she said, after thinking it over for a minute. "That seems fair."

"I'm so glad you approve."

A few days later, she hoped he meant those words when Tyler returned to the bar after a bank appointment to find that she'd fired Jack in his absence.

"You what?"

She'd acted at the time without thinking, and knowing that made her even more uncomfortable now.

"I only did what you would have done. He was over an hour late, he didn't call, and I fired him."

"You fired him."

Hurrying on, before Tyler could threaten her with the fate she'd recently dealt out to young Jack, she continued, "But don't worry, we've got a new waitress coming in for training tonight. We'll be fine."

"You fired Jack, and you hired someone? Who?"

Even to her own ears, this was sounding worse and worse.

"That girl you interviewed last week. Anita."

She could see him trying to remember, and the expression on his face when he did was not pleasant. "That girl? She was so nervous talking to me I could hardly make heads or tails of anything she said. Have you completely lost your mind?"

"Of course not. But we chatted after you were through." She lost some of her nervousness at this point. One thing she knew she did well was hire staff. That she had no real right to do so at this restaurant was irrelevant, she told herself. "She was scared because she really wants this job. She needs it. I'll train her and she'll knock herself out to do a good job, Tyler. I promise you."

"I don't know why I even bother coming in anymore. You're running this place just fine without me," he grumbled as he walked behind the bar.

"Sorry. I know I overstepped my bounds today." She tried to look sheepish, which seemed to amuse Tyler more than anything else.

"I ought to fire your butt," he said. Then he leaned over the bar, grabbed her face and attacked her mouth with soft, nipping kisses. She felt the roller coaster dip of sex bloom in her stomach and opened her mouth to his. His tongue tangled with hers and then he pulled away slowly, sucking gently on the curve of her bottom lip. "But you'd probably stop sleeping with me." As she sputtered, he went on. "Besides, you did the right thing. If Anita drives all my customers away with her stuttering, though, I'm taking it out on your hide.''

She grinned, relieved that she was getting off so easy.

"Promise?"

"Witch. Get to work." He snapped a bar towel at her and jerked his head at a table of newcomers.

From that moment on, although Grace managed to refrain from taking any similarly large liberties with Tyler's business, she knew he wouldn't be fazed by anything she did on the job. Privately, the incident seemed to somehow bring them closer, too.

One Sunday morning, she made him pancakes for breakfast, letting him laugh at how closely she read the instructions on the box.

"You thought I was kidding about the no-cooking-without-a-recipe thing," she said, and laughed as Tyler's guilty look confirmed it. "Don't worry. As long as the recipe's in English or—well, I promise not to poison you." She turned her back on him and leaned over her pans on the stovetop. Catching herself before saying *Or in French* was all well and good, but sooner or later she'd let something slip that would force Tyler to question her more closely.

"I'll take my chances," he murmured in her ear, stepping up against her back and tucking her hair aside to kiss her neck. Her hands shook as she poured the batter into the sizzling pan, spattering pancake polka dots across the hot surface. Her neck arched involuntarily as his hand skimmed up her side to cup her breast beneath the T-shirt she'd stolen off him. She searched for his mouth with her own as he leaned over her shoulder, her hands fumbling blindly at the range top dials to shut the damn stove off.

She twisted frantically in his arms and attacked him. His hands under her bare bottom urged her up and with a jump she wrapped herself around him, legs hooked around his waist.

"Pancakes." She said the word in between kisses.

"Some other time," he muttered as he walked with her out of the kitchen, heading to the bedroom.

"Mmm, hmm." She was too busy running her mouth and her hands over every inch of his bare skin she could reach to answer.

After he left for the restaurant, she called her attorney. The meeting had been arranged for the following week.

"Call them back and make it for Friday noon. And anyone who can't make it will be notified by mail as to the results. I can't take this much longer."

"But, Ms. Haley—"

"Don't argue with me, Franklin. Just make it happen."

With seventy-two hours to go before her meeting, Grace began having a little trouble. The near slip while cooking breakfast was the beginning of a string of incidents in which she slid closer to the tricky slope of revealing herself by her words and actions.

When her alma mater won its first basketball game of the season and she shouted out "Go Stanford!" to a bar packed with customers, she blamed it on wishful thinking.

"Always thought it would be great to go to school there." And smacked herself in the forehead as soon as she escaped to the bathroom.

Grace stared at her face in the mirror. "Just be Grace Desmond for a few more days. Grace Desmond, that's all."

But it was no use. All Autumn long, Grace had submerged her own personality in the role as much as possible, so that she'd only occasionally had to question her reactions. Now, with the return to her own life imminent, and so much of her time spent strategizing for that return, she was finding it even more difficult to keep Grace Haley shut up in a box. It seemed that she could not turn her own personality on and off like a faucet. To act as Grace Haley part of the time, apparently meant that her instincts would lead her to respond as Grace Haley at anytime.

And her judgment was shot. She could no longer tell what was harmless and what was dangerously inappropriate behavior on her part. Second-guessing herself was becoming a habit, but now she started questioning herself for questioning herself.

I'm going crazy here, and it's going to be hard to miss. The best I can do is to try to minimize the damage. I can't avoid Tyler. Aside from the fact that I don't *want* to avoid him, we work together, and sleep together. Makes that whole avoidance thing a bit tricky, no? But I can stay away from him during the day, and watch my mouth the rest of the time.

So she shut up.

If Tyler thought it was strange that she started leaving his apartment before he did each morning, he said nothing about it. And he didn't seem to notice that she avoided entering into conversations with him unless they were work-related, which frankly she found a little annoying.

Sarah did notice however, and cornered Grace Wednesday night in the kitchen.

"What's up with you, Grace? You haven't said more than ten words to me since you got here tonight. And I notice you're not exactly chatting with my brother, either. What's wrong?"

"Nothing," Grace said. She saw by Sarah's shake of her head that she wasn't being particularly convincing, and repeated herself. "Really, it's nothing." She grabbed the tubful of dirty dishes that Sarah had forgotten to put down out of her roommate's arms and lugged it over to the dish room. "I've been thinking a lot lately about my family. I'm trying to figure out what to do. How to make sure the right thing happens." She turned and flashed a grin at Sarah, ignoring the tug of guilt she felt as she used knowledge gained from their growing friendship to change the subject. "It's not like I'm spending my time trying to plot ways to do away with my boyfriend."

"Ex!" Sarah's shout had her mother turning from the stove where she was attempting to train a new cook how to make her special pesto sauce. Grace didn't know if Susannah's recipe was especially complicated, if the new cook was less bright than he seemed, or if Tyler's mother was more reluctant to give up her position in the kitchen than she wanted to admit. In any case, Sarah lowered her voice. "And I am not plotting to do away with him."

"Mmm, hmm?"

"Fantasizing out loud about shutting him up in one of the clinic's dog cages and poking him with a sharp stick until he begs for mercy is not plotting." Sarah slammed the door down on the dishwasher and poked the start button with stiff, accusatory fingers. "Can you believe that bastard told me he doesn't see why we can't continue working together?"

"I don't understand why you still are, frankly," Grace said, spraying hot water on the waiting tub of dishes. "It would serve him right to be left high and dry if you never showed up again."

"I know," Sarah said grimly. She attacked a scorched pot that had been soaking in the sink. "But finding a good veterinary assistant isn't as easy as you might think. And I am not going to have those animals suffer poor quality of care, just because my *ex*-boyfriend is a low-life, lying, scheming, idiot *married* schmuck!"

The laughter Grace had strapped down burst out of her.

Sarah threatened her with a spray from the hot water hose and Grace threw up her hands in self-defense, still laughing.

"Wait! It's just because you're so fierce." She started to lower her hands and then thought better of giving Sarah a free shot. "I was afraid you were going to be depressed for ages when you told me. You'd already seemed to be upset about things with him in the past."

"Yeah, well, I was upset because I thought *I* was doing something stupid by dating my boss." Her laugh was genuine. "Now that I know he's an even bigger idiot, I'm just pissed."

"Good. I'll sharpen the stick for you."

"I think my brother's beaten you to it."

"I'm just happy he hasn't been arrested yet for intention to cause bodily harm. He was ready to tear the guy's heart out when he heard." A shout from the front of the bar let her escape while Sarah was distracted by the pleasing thought of Tyler vivisecting her ex-boyfriend. And escape was essential, because Grace most definitely did not want to think about how angry Tyler was that his sister had been lied to.

She was already stressing enough about the idea of confessing her multitude of deceptions to Tyler and his family. She didn't think she could take the thought of all of them comparing her to the slimeball who'd just admitted to lying to Sarah about his marital status. Pile lying about her name, occupation, financial situation, and general history on top of the fact that most of Chicago high society considered her as good as married, and she thought that Sarah's ex might come off pretty good in comparison.

Push it out of your mind, girl. There's still a job to be done tonight.

At the front of the house, her party of twenty had arrived and were milling about in confusion. Reeling off directions to the coatrack and the bathrooms, Grace began herding everyone to the large table she'd assembled along the wall. Ten minutes later, after serving all twenty people drinks, no two of which were the same, and scattering plates of preordered appetizers about the table, the party rhythm was flowing nicely, and Grace waved Tyler off from covering for her at another table. She headed back to the bar a minute later and called out her order.

"Glenlivet up, Stoli rocks, splash of tonic and a water back." Streams of liquor arced between bottle and glass, tonic and water shot from the soda gun, and her order was ready. She eyed the bar setup critically. "You know, if you installed another soda gun on this side of the wait station, your servers could save you some time. Since you're the only bartender, you shouldn't waste time pouring sodas."

Tyler shook his head, but waited to answer until she returned from distributing the drinks. "You're just trying to conceal your caffeine addiction from the world, you diet cola-guzzling fiend. At least now I can keep track of how many you ask me to pour you, and nag you about it."

"It's mother's milk to me, I swear."

"It's bad for you, I swear. Particularly when you make it a fifth food group."

Grace grinned, stood on tiptoe, craned her arm around the napkin holder and snagged the soda gun with two fingers. She pushed a button and poured herself a diet Coke, then fumbled the gun back into the holder screwed onto the inner edge of the counter.

Tyler's eyes narrowed with menace. "Exactly how long have you been able to pull that trick?"

"Since my first day," she said. The arm he cocked in preparation for a throw was loaded with a dirty bar rag. "Hey! I hardly ever use it! It's more fun listening to you scold me."

"C'mere." He beckoned her in closer. Wary, she leaned over the counter.

His hand snaked around the back of her neck and tugged her all the way to his mouth. His other palm cupped her cheek as Tyler covered her lips with his own in a long, luxurious kiss that set her skin on fire. He let her go, fingertips trailing along her jaw, and Grace slid her elbows off the bar and fell back onto her feet. Dazzled.

Loud noise poked at her awareness. Hearing and vision, outside of the closed circle of her and Tyler, returned in a rush of cheers and clapping hands. One of their regulars started whacking the side of his glass with a spoon, the age-old signal for the bride and groom to kiss at the reception.

"Way to go, Gracie!"

"Never thought I'd see Tyler in love!"

"Give it up, ladies! The man is most definitely off the market!"

Tyler let his gaze rest gently on Grace, looking for the inevitable blush that flamed over her face every time he made a show of affection for her in public.

Grabbing her tray and hefting it onto her shoulders, she started to swing away from the bar and back to her table, until Tyler caught her eye. Was he worried about the regulars' gossip? Or about the fact that she'd consistently tried to hide their relationship from everyone around them? It didn't matter anymore. She was too close to freedom, to telling the truth about everything. Why shouldn't everyone know about the two of them now?

Lifting her free hand in the air and raising her brows, she

mouthed the words, *If you can't beat them...* at him and blew him a kiss.

"Better hang a sign 'round his neck, Gracie. Try, This Table Reserved!"

The loudest guffaw ringing out behind her seemed to come from Tyler himself. Funny man.

Two hours later, he was still smiling behind the bar, overflowing with even more good humor than usual. Grace wondered what he was up to. He seemed to be taking every opportunity to touch her in little, lover-like ways, brief caresses of her hands or face, quick kisses on her fingertips or anything else he could get his hands on. And if he winked at her any more often, he'd get a cramp in his eye.

She called out her order and enjoyed the moment of standing still while she waited. When Tyler slid the drinks onto her tray, she flushed at the sight of his fingers sliding off the glasses, wet with condensation, and immediately felt silly.

"And what are you thinking that makes you blush, love?" Even his voice was seducing her, damn it.

Grace looked up in time to see, over Tyler's shoulder—*and what distracting shoulders*—what looked like, but clearly could not be, the Taco Bell Chihuahua arcing through the air over her party's table. She blinked hard and squinted.

"Grace?" She knew confusion was written all over her face as she stepped away from the bar. "What is it?"

"Flying...dog?"

Before she took three steps, however, yet another object was launched over the table. This time the missile seemed to be a large ball of pink cashmere, topped with a pile of fluffy peach hair. Seconds later, all hell broke loose.

High-pitched yapping noises from beneath the table confirmed the canine presence. The pink and peach ball of fluff landed on a man in a blue suit talking on a cell phone, and started shrieking, "You killed my Poopsie! My Poopsie!" Chairs clattered to the floor as men and women jumped to their feet and rushed to the battle.

"Hold it!" Grace dove into the fray and laid hands on anything she could grab. Something clocked her in the temple; she strongly suspected the suit of fighting back with his only weapon. She came up from the floor with a wildly flailing woman in one hand and a terrorized, near-sobbing man in another. People pressed closely around her. "Back off! Everyone sit down!"

Placing herself squarely between the combatants, she kept her hands fisted in both shirtfronts. Out of the corner of her eye, she sensed Tyler standing a few feet away, glowering at everyone, a growling Chihuahua trapped in his hands.

"You—" she shook the businessman "—stop crying and tell me what happened. You shut up," she added to the strawberry-blonde, who seemed to being having a difficult time remaining upright. She let go of the man, needing both hands to prop up the tipsy woman.

"She…she attacked me," he stuttered, stuffing his shirt back inside his pants and then drying his eyes on his cuffs. "And that was after the rat jumped in my lap. What kind of place is this?"

"Poor—" hiccup "—Poopsie."

"She's hammered," came a helpful voice from the crowd.

And everything slid into place.

She silenced the crowd with a few sharp words, sent Anita running to the kitchen and started explaining.

"We have no, let me repeat, *no,* rodent problems at Tyler's. We do however seem to have a *small* problem with dogs tonight, no pun intended." Tyler lifted the still yapping dog in the air and Grace saw a few smiles. Feeling like Hercule Poirot at the end of an Agatha Christie novel, she continued. "Someone—" she stared pointedly at the woman who looked about to collapse into a liquid pool "—apparently thought her little darling should enjoy the party tonight, and things seem to have gotten a little out of hand."

"Nice going, Marlene," someone shouted.

She exhaled deeply. The mutters surging through the small crowd appeared to be shifting focus to the dog smuggler. From the back of the house, she saw Anita approaching, an enormous tray balanced on her shoulder.

"To make up for any momentary interruption to your evening, Tyler's would like to offer everyone a drink on the house, and Anita is here with a fabulous selection of treats from our amazing chef. I know you all enjoyed your dinners. I can promise you that you will absolutely love your desserts." Several women turned immediately and descended on Anita, who looked frightened at their stalking approach.

"If you'll excuse me, I'm going to get our friend Marlene here some coffee. And a cab."

So saying, Grace slung the woman's limp arm around her shoulder and half walked, half dragged her over to the wait station and poured her into a chair.

"Nice crowd control," came Tyler's voice from behind her.

"Thanks. Always better to cough up some free drinks than have people talking about your 'rat' problem."

"True, but this woman is beyond over-served. How'd you let that happen?"

Barely noticing that the tension, just beginning to drain from her muscles, surged right back into place, she snapped back at Tyler, "I didn't. She ordered two whiskey rocks in three hours, and no one else bought one for her. She should be fine. What else did you have to drink tonight?" The last she barked at the intoxicted woman.

"I jus' had a li'l." Marlene's tongue seemed to be getting in the way of her mouth.

"A little what, Marlene?"

"A li'l of everything," she giggled, and then frowned. Grace thought she was trying to look stern. "*Some* people don' know howda finish their drinks. S'a shame." She shook her head woefully.

"What's the commotion?" Sarah popped up next to them, drying her hands on her apron. "Sounded like World War Three out here."

"Well, little Miss Marlene here has apparently been sucking

down the dregs of every cocktail she found abandoned within reach for the last three hours,'' Grace told her.

"Gross."

"Yes it is. And the rest we can pretty much blame on her little rat dog here."

Tyler raised the dog again, Marlene sucked in a deep breath—*preparing to roast me, no doubt*—for the rat comment, and Poopsie decided she'd had enough. She turned her head and bit the only thing in reach. Tyler. Who promptly dropped the dog and grabbed his wounded hand.

"Goddamn it!"

"Poopsie!"

"Not again," Grace muttered as she lunged after Marlene. The woman was trying to throttle Tyler. Grace thrust a hand in the fluffy peach hair and yanked, hard. Marlene spun around swinging.

"No fighting!" Still conscious of the other patrons in the bar, Grace trapped the crazy lady's arms at her sides and aimed her low shout directly into one bejeweled ear. "There is no fighting in my bar. Do you understand me?" she demanded.

In the back of her mind, she knew that Tyler and Sarah could both hear her instinctive claim to ownership and authority, but she couldn't be worried about that. She knew for herself what her words meant.

The woman stopped struggling and arched her neck back to hiss spitefully.

"This isn't your place. He's the owner here." Her lascivious eyes lowered in an attempt at flirtation toward Tyler. "You're just a *waitress*."

Shoving the woman back into the nearby chair, Grace loomed over her, power and pride and anger racing through her veins like a flood of cold fire, until her eyes burned in a mask of ice. Leaning forward, she pressed the woman back with the sheer force of her presence. She thrust one finger to within millimeters of Marlene's red nose.

"When I am on the floor, it's my house. And I do not tol-erate brawling in my house," she enunciated slowly and distinctly. Marlene's eyes were fixated on the stabbing finger. "Are we clear on that? Because if not, I will become the *waitress* who will call the cops on you for drunk and disorderly."

The woman nodded. It seemed all she was capable of.

Still hot, Grace turned and fixed Tyler in place with the same finger, his mouth open with words she would not allow to tumble from his lips. "And you…"

He shut his mouth.

"You should know better than to think that I would *let* something like this happen." The hurt she'd ignored at his earlier, blaming words came back to her. Echoes of her mother and Charles, accusing her of causing them trouble rang in her mind. She'd thought he knew her better. And in her guilty knowledge that his ignorance was due to her duplicity, she struck out. "How could you even think that I would allow anything to hurt your business, to hurt you, if I could possibly prevent it? I would never do that. Never."

Dropping her arm, she stood still, breathing heavily. She was surrounded by the silence of shock, in Sarah, in the drunken woman, in Tyler.

And in that silence, another sound crept on mice feet into her awareness. The sound of trickling water, rising from the floor beneath her feet, barely audible under the rollicking music of the Clancy Brothers. She looked down.

Poopsie stood spread-eagled over the toe of her right shoe, looking guiltily up at her as pee streamed over leather. The dog let out an apologetic whine.

"Grace."

She held up her hands.

"Not now." Deep breaths. "Anita can cover my tables. I'm going for a walk. To cool down."

Grabbing a handful of beverage napkins off the bar and some ice wrapped in a towel, she stepped slowly out of the puddle of dog pee, turned, and stalked out.

Outside, the cool night air was a soothing hand on her skin, gently stroking the heat away. She exhaled slowly, breathing out her anger and frustration with herself, and held the lumpy, cold towel to her temple. It was ridiculous to let herself get this worked up. All this trouble over a dog. At the thought of Poopsie she sighed and dropped her glance to her shoe.

She walked away from the lights of the doorway and over to the curb, where she sat in the even darker shade of a tree whose night-shadowed leaves blocked the light of the street-lamps. Dipping a napkin into a puddle left in the gutter by the recent rain, she began carefully blotting her shoe, patting automatically as her mind wandered and ached, overwhelmed with tiredness and guilt.

I should have noticed what was going on. Tyler was right. Even if I didn't know how it was happening, I should have noticed before now that that woman needed to go home. Not to mention my stellar lack of observation in regard to the canine invasion that had apparently been going on right in front of me. And I would have, too, if I weren't spending so much of my time mooning over Tyler and worrying about my own problems. I wasn't doing my job, because I was too wrapped up with myself.

Which wasn't fair to Tyler, the one person who'd done nothing but help her. It wasn't fair to his family, either, every one of whom was putting in time at the restaurant on top of their own jobs.

She braced her elbows on her knees and stared into the street.

Maybe it would be better if she left. Better for everyone.

Matters would, of course, become extremely hectic at the restaurant without her, but wasn't that simply going to be even more true the longer she stayed? The more important she became to Tyler, and the more responsibility she took on at the pub, the bigger the gaping hole left behind once she was gone. And that she would be gone, soon, was not a question but a certainty. Her business, *her* business, needed her. She refused to watch everything her grandmother had worked for be frittered away by her mother and Charles on parties and clothes and easy living. She refused to let fear of them make her as irresponsible as they were. That, she would not allow.

She pushed herself to her feet and wiped the grit off her palms.

It was time to tell the truth.

She'd been dreading this moment for so long that the decision to confess was like finally getting stuck in the arm with a hypodermic needle. The pain was so much less overwhelming than the anxiety leading up to it that it actually felt like sweet relief. It was time to stop being such a scaredy-cat. She would tell Tyler. He would forgive her or he would not. Either way, she would leave. She could send one of her staff over to replace her, wages to be paid by the Haley Group, because she knew she owed him a debt and she would repay it. And maybe someday, when she had more of a grip on her life, she could come back. To see how things were going without her. To say hi.

Yanking the heavy front door open, she stepped inside the pub and headed straight for the bar. This was too important, and she didn't trust herself to wait.

She was pulled up short by a clutching hand on her sleeve and turned to find Anita desperately blinking back tears.

"Sweetie, what is it?"

"I—I—I need—" the girl gulped and dragged her sleeve across her wet eyes "—and…and there's a man…who won't—" she snuffled "—and the dog is still…" She wailed, "Oh, Grace, please help me!"

Grace glanced at the bar and spotted Tyler holding off a siege of his own. He had two pitchers and six pints filling under the taps, three shakers on the bar rail, awaiting shaking and dripping condensation from their contents, and two blenders running for frozen margaritas. She caught his eye, and had no problem reading his lips.

Help her! Please!

"Okay," she said, turning a bright grin on the hyperventilating Anita. "Deep breaths. Let's get this all straightened out. I'll take care of the dog and the man who won't…whatever. You just go get what you need."

Teary thanks, a small, grateful smile, and Grace was back

in the thick of things. "I need to talk to you," she told Tyler in the middle of one trip to the bar for more cocktails.

"I know. Me, too. Later?"

She nodded and threw herself back into the fray.

Restaurants being restaurants, and all the same no matter where they are, needing a moment to talk to the boss was as much a guarantee of high-volume business as ordering something to eat during the first five minutes of quiet after ten hours on the floor. The customers kept streaming in the front door, and although Grace was happy to hear the symphony of profit playing on the cash register bell, her own plans swirled right down the drain with the excess beer spillage under the taps.

By 2:00 a.m., she was exhausted, cranky and craving sleep with a need bordering on psychosis. She'd sent Anita home more than an hour earlier, with instructions to make some decaffeinated tea, perhaps with a slug of whiskey in it, watch some terrible late-night television and go to sleep. She'd also promised that the girl would never have to go through another night like this one.

Stripping off her apron and depositing it on a small table, she trudged up to the bar to turn in her checks and cash.

"Paperwork for Anita and me checks out, Tyler."

"Great. Thanks," he replied, bent over his own drawer and stack of charge slips. After a second, the flatness of Grace's voice registered with his tired brain and he glanced over his shoulder.

She'd slid herself onto a bar stool and rested her cheek on one hand, and promptly fallen asleep. Crossing to her, Tyler could see the bruise on her temple, and her fragilely bluish eyelids fluttering restlessly. He knew her well enough to be certain that she was telling herself to open her eyes, that she was still awake. He cursed her mentally for working herself to this point of exhaustion, until the obvious corollary occurred to him.

You jerk, he thought with rising embarrassment, she's only doing it for you. And you let her drain herself dry right in front of you. Some boyfriend—some boss—you make.

He stretched out a hand and brushed it gently over her hair. Strands had escaped from all over the elegant twist she'd made of her heavy blond hair. The loose waves skimming her cheek would tickle if she were awake.

Softly, he pushed the hair out of her face and brought his hand back to trace the slight arch of her brow. His Grace. He'd seen her at every hour of day and night, and in a mad variety of situations. Seen her face animated with every emotion, and every moment was printed indelibly on his memories.

Brows lowered, eyes narrowed to mere slits, jaw clenching rhythmically with enormous anger and yet supreme self-control.

Eyes narrowed again, this time because she was laughing, and her free expression of joy shone in her face in a wide grin that flushed her cheeks and crinkled her usually invisible laugh lines.

The special looks, reserved for Tyler alone, that melted like liquid wax over his skin, bringing the heat instantly to the surface, mirroring Grace's flush as she saw each time how immediately he responded to her eyes.

Her free hand rested on the bar. Tyler placed it gently in his own. He could feel where the warmth of her hand had left its heat in the smooth varnish of the wood bar.

"Grace."

"Mumph."

"Grace."

"Awake."

"You're asleep." He pressed a twenty-dollar bill into her lax palm. "Go home. You still have the spare key. There's a cab out front. I'll be right behind you."

"Hmm. 'Kay," she mumbled, and then slowly pried her eyes open. "What's that?"

"Bedtime, baby."

He walked her to the door, wrapping her in her jacket and then watching as she shuffled her way to the waiting taxi. The cab pulled away from the curb and he locked the door behind her.

The click of the lock fell muffled into the dying silence of the room. A soft rattle from the back heralded the dumping of a fresh tray in the ice machine. The everyday noises of the building continued. The hum of the spinning brushes for glass-washing behind the bar. The near-subliminal rumbling of the high-tech, smoke-eating ventilation system. Even the jukebox still floated Billie Holiday at low volume throughout the room. Only, to Tyler, it all seemed as flat as three-day-old 7Up.

I'm in love with her.

In the quiet bar, with all of the life fled from the room, just because she was gone, it was achingly clear.

I am in love with Grace.

As important as everything else in his life was, his family, his business, it all paled in comparison with this overwhelming need he felt: to love her, take care of her, and know that she would always be there to look him straight in the eye and love him back.

Fifteen minutes later—paperwork be damned—he shoved his spare key into the lock to his home and snapped it open. Kicking off his shoes as he went, he arrowed straight to his bedroom.

The flood of warmth at the sight of Grace curled up in his bed stopped him at the door. With one arm flung across all of the pillows and the other hand snuggled carefully beneath her cheek, she laid claim to the space as if she belonged there.

Tyler knew she did.

Sliding next to her into bed, he gathered her carefully in his arms and whispered nonsense at her until she awoke. Reluctantly, her eyes opened, looking dazedly around her until her gaze tangled with his and a slow smile broke over her face like dawn.

"Hey." Her word was barely audible as she kissed him sleepily.

"I love you, Grace." Her smile stretched even wider as she tilted her head back and closed her eyes, presumably in joy.

He knew this was a bit of a shock to her, but he wasn't done yet.

"I love you, Grace," he repeated, and then put his lips up to her ear. "And I want you to be my partner in the pub."

Nine

She was having the most amazing dream.

Wrapped in warmth, the soft murmur of her lover's voice whispering in her ear, she reveled in the security that enveloped her, the love that surrounded her. Love. He slid his lips along her cheekbone, raining kisses on her face, and she knew she loved him. She tilted her head back as his mouth wandered to her throat and...

...spoke of contracts?

Visions of clouds and soft sunlight vanished into a rolling screen of legal documents, all bearing Tyler's name and her own, surrounding Grace's dream haven.

She opened her eyes.

Tyler leaned above her, a satisfied grin on his face. Clearly he was waiting for a response from her. Unfortunately, she had no idea what was going on.

"Did you say something?" Maybe she could buy time.

A slight frown shifted his face. "Didn't you hear me?"

She bit her lip and tried not to look guilty as she shook her head no. She hadn't heard him, or at least she hoped she hadn't. But she was very afraid that he'd said something dangerous.

"You spoke to me," he said, slightly accusing.

"I've been known to have entire conversations with people while still sleeping," she whispered, and leaned up to kiss him. Maybe distraction would work better. "Sorry. I'm awake now." She snaked her arms around his neck and pulled his face back to hers. Sinking deep into the kiss, she gave herself over to the soul-destroying feeling of his mouth on hers. Her hands fisted in his hair as desire crackled like brushfire through her body.

Tyler's open mouth scraped against hers fiercely as his own hands raced up her sides to close with devastating familiarity over her breasts. He fit her so well. Every touch of his body on hers was as natural as if they'd been making love for years, and yet each moment was an aching burst of new amazement that he could make her feel like this. Treasured and gentle, fierce and demanding.

A moment later he pulled his mouth from hers. He manacled her wrists in his hands and pulled them away from his body to trap her beneath him on the bed.

"I can't believe I'm saying this, but we have to stop." He groaned the words out between harsh breaths.

"I don't see why," she answered, wrapping a leg around his waist and clamping him to her. She arched her pelvis to press herself hard against him. Uncontrollably, a short moan ʊroke in the back of her throat.

"Grace, I love you." He slid his hands up her arms until he cradled her face, and his eyes shone above her in the dim light. "I love you."

Joy exploded like sun in her heart. She blinked sudden tears from her eyes and her hands trembled as she laid her hands against his. Love drowned out the voice in her head telling her, *No, no, this is too soon. He can't say this yet. He doesn't know.*

"Please tell me you're crying from happiness," he said, his voice low and unsteady.

"Yes, oh, yes." The tears fell. Her throat ached. "It's just that sometimes you can be so much in love with someone that it makes your heart hurt.''

She kissed him, blindly, over and over again, repeating the words, loving him so desperately in this moment that all of her lies and fears didn't matter. Her mouth sought his, begging reassurance, claiming forgiveness for all the hurt she would yet cause him. She read the confusion in his body as he tried to pull away from her.

''Grace? What's wrong?''

She didn't answer, determined to love him so much in this one moment that he would never forget it, no matter what happened.

''Shh.'' She pressed a finger to his lips, then let it drift softly to the corner of his mouth. Teased the crease there until his mouth opened and turned in search of her fingers, which she pulled away to run across the ridge of his brow and then drift down over his eyelids, closing them softly. She trailed her hands gently down the entire length of his face, each sensitive pad of her fingertips registering the slightest change in the curves and valleys of his face, until she was running her hands down his neck and over his shoulders, still feather-light.

With a sudden push of her palms, she rolled Tyler off her and over onto his back as she propped herself up on one arm and gazed at him. He kept his eyes open this time and she skimmed his features again, traced a finger lightly over his ear, outlined his jaw, dragged her hand softly down his cheek. When he started to speak, she hushed him again and sat up beside him.

''Shh.'' She started painting the muscles of his shoulders and arms with the sensitized pads of her fingertips, moving slowly, barely touching him, drifting over and over every square inch of his arms.

''I'm memorizing you,'' she said, and barely registered the huskiness of her own voice. His body twitched at her words and then she felt him deliberately relax beside her.

She made her way down his chest next, still using only her fingers on his skin. Though when she leaned over him and the tips of her hair brushed against his skin and Tyler's back arced reflexively, she allowed herself a little smile.

His stomach quivered beneath her hands, his hips rocking slightly and his breathing growing harsh as she neared his sex.

And passed it, moving the air a millimeter from his skin, but not touching him where every fiber of his being craved her hands, her mouth.

Tyler felt as though she was tearing the soul from his body, inch by inch.

When she skimmed a fingertip over the sensitive skin at the top of his thigh, where his leg met his hip, Tyler's harsh gasp startled her into glancing up at his face.

The tendons in his neck stood out sharply, visible proof of the control he was exerting over himself to simply lie still while she touched him.

Long, shallow indentations ran down his thighs, sharply defining the muscles there and fascinating her for several minutes, until she found the silklike skin at the back of his knees and lingered there for a while. The ridge of his calf muscles was next, and the straightness of his shins, trailing down into ankles that were surprisingly ticklish.

And with each stroke of her fingers over his skin, she took him into herself, memorized his every texture, every hard angle and gentle slope of his body, and knew she would never forget any of this. With each stroke of her fingers, she could feel his hands tracing the same paths over her skin, as she knew he wanted to.

The ghosts of his fingers curling around the roundness of her arms, stroking down her breasts, across her stomach, tracing the length of her legs, and finally nearing the core of her hunger for him. As she stroked her way back up his legs to the center of his wanting for her.

One of her legs draped across his thighs, the other curled beneath her, she leaned over him. At last. Still her fingertips barely touched him as she moved her hand up the silky, strong length of him. There was moisture, which pleased her and she painted it in slick circles over the tip.

"I'll never forget this," she murmured, and her warm breath on his sex nearly undid him.

Then her mouth closed over him, and he was undone. Lost in the heat of her, in the dazzling sensation of feeling each touch of her hands on his body, every inch of her memorization, burst into flaming awareness. A tracery of light mapped out over his body and burning now, as her mouth set him on fire.

Tyler's control snapped. With a savage yank, he dragged Grace up his body, locked his mouth on hers and thrust deeply into her.

And as his body rose into hers, she clung to him. Wrapped herself around him and held on as her soul raced to meet his in a crash of light and love and shuddering bursts of pleasure that pounded through her.

Grace drifted slowly back to herself. Tyler's weight was a sensuous heaviness pressing her into the bed. Then he rolled onto his back with a groan, pulling her with him to lay sprawled across his body. His eyes were still closed as he spoke.

"I should have told you I loved you ages ago."

His eyes blinked open and he looked up at her, an exhausted smile barely lifting the corners of his mouth. He pushed sweat-damp hair behind her ears and she arched her neck into the touch of his hands. She was still without words.

"It was just so clear. After you left the bar tonight. That I'm only completely happy when you're with me. So I knew."

But was love supposed to be like this? Grace wondered, as her heart broke wide open. To be so perfect in its beauty that it caused pain? She rested her head on Tyler's chest and traced the words of her happiness on his bare skin with her fingertip.

I love you.

"Me, too." He crushed her to him. "God, Grace. Me, too. You're the best thing that's ever happened to me." His breath moved her hair. "Not to mention my business. I was prepared to fail, completely and totally. And I was prepared to succeed beyond my wildest dreams and go crazy trying to solve all the problems brought by that success.''

He lifted her head off his chest and focused on her.

''But I never thought it could happen so easily, so smoothly. Because I didn't know there was someone out there to be strong where I might be weak. To solve problems before I even imagined they existed. Someone I could rely on and trust to back me up, in everything. You're an amazing woman, Grace, and I don't think you know that. I don't think you know how incredibly talented you are, but I'm going to keep telling you until you believe it.''

With his words, the light went out. Her body felt numb and cold and she wondered that Tyler couldn't feel the chill radiating out from her skin, from her heart.

Because it was lies. All of it, lies. She did know her own talents, But Tyler did not. He didn't know anything about her. About the life she was even now plotting to get back for herself. For the right reasons, of course, but the fact that he didn't know any of it turned all of the shiny golden glow of his words into muddy dross.

Talented, was she? Well, with a degree from Stanford, an M.B.A. from Kellogg and a lifetime spent working in her family's conglomerate of restaurants, she certainly ought to be. Of course, Tyler thought she was a diner waitress making good, probably with a high-school education. He could be proud of her, because he only knew enough about her to make her look good.

How much would he love her if he knew she'd been lying to him since the day she'd walked in the door of the pub? How proud would he be, if he knew that she'd run away from her own responsibilities and obligations, leaving hundreds of people employed by the Haley Group in danger of losing their jobs? She didn't think he'd find her so amazing if he knew the truth.

And if her dream earlier was any indication, things were about to get worse.

''Tyler, listen, I'm not what you think—''

"Stop. You are." His finger pressed lightly on her lips. "You're smart and capable and beautiful and caring. And I want you to be my partner. You called it your restaurant earlier tonight, and I want that to be true even when you're not on the floor."

She started to protest, but he talked over her words.

"I know you won't just let me give it to you. So we'll set something up where you can buy into the business gradually, over time, until you're a full partner. Meanwhile, everything will just keep going like it is now."

"Stop! Just stop," she interrupted, rolling off of him. Knowing that she could buy his business with the funds in her smallest money market account only made things worse. The sheets were twisted beneath them. She pulled at a cover in frustration until she could wrap it around herself and get out of bed. Being naked felt too vulnerable right now.

The blanket trailed behind her as she paced, tripping her when she turned to face the bed. Tyler was sitting up, leaning against the headboard. He looked calm, but clearly disappointed.

"Tyler, there's so much you don't know about me," she began, and then stopped as the gross understatement threw her off stride. She wrapped the blanket more tightly around herself and shifted her weight nervously from one foot to the other. If she had a free hand, she knew she'd be reflexively tugging on her hair at that moment.

"You're right," he said steadily. "But I know you're afraid of something, or someone. Hell, I'd have started with a marriage proposal instead of a business one, if I didn't think that would scare you off for good." He grinned.

"Don't joke," she snapped, and saw instantly by the hurt in his eyes that he hadn't been. She closed her eyes for a moment and stood silent. A night for many pains, apparently. "I'm sorry. I don't know how I let things get so out of control. I'm a mess, Tyler. And the last thing I want to do is to hurt you or disappoint you."

"You won't."

"Don't say that. You can't know that."

"You said the same thing to me earlier tonight. It was true then and it's true now. I don't know who you were, but I know who you are now, Grace. You would never hurt me."

"I don't want to. But I'm afraid I will."

There were miles between her and Tyler, continents with unassailable mountain ranges and unbridgeable crevasses. In the middle of the room, she felt very alone. The gap between them seemed impossible to cross. If only he'd waited until she was free to tell him everything. Free to come to him as a woman in charge of her own life.

But now she couldn't even remember why she'd decided to wait. She knew in an instant that she'd made a terrible mistake. Tyler would have been able to handle anything she could have thrown at him. But not now. Not when he'd just laid his heart bare in his trust for her. She couldn't say anything right now without shattering that moment.

"Maybe I'd better go."

She turned to collect her clothes, only to be caught by the naked roughness of his voice.

"Please. Stay."

His words called to her. The moonlight spilled through the uncurtained window to skim a glow along the outline of his arm as he stretched a hand out to her.

"December thirty-first, remember? No questions asked until then. Just stay."

It was wrong. With every breath she took in, she knew that it was wrong to stay with Tyler under such blatantly false pretenses. She knew that she risked everything, including his hatred when he found out the truth, if she continued to be with him now. She had so much to lose.

Her body moved toward him, pulled by the force of his desire, his love, and she didn't stop herself. It was unthinkable to leave. Her hand found itself clasped and a final tug pulled her neatly to his side, where she'd found so much security such a brief time before. She felt anything but secure now.

"I want to help you, Grace."

"You can't help me with this." Her body arced to merge with his. "Just love me. Love me no matter what."

His promise was written in the strokes of his hands on her skin and he loved her as she wept.

Standing at the door of the penthouse suite at the Drake Hotel, her hand clammy on the doorknob, she held the memory of Tyler's loving in her mind and took strength from it. Her heartbeat slowed, her thoughts stopped racing around in circles, her muscles unclenched. Two deep breaths and she opened the door.

Conversation halted instantly and heads swiveled toward her as the thirteen men and women in the room rose to their feet.

"Good afternoon. Thank you for agreeing to this impromptu meeting, particularly on such short notice. If you'll all take your seats, please, I'd like to get right down to business."

Her voice remained calm and steady, she was pleased to note as she moved to the head of the conference table around which they all sat themselves.

"I've asked you all here to clear up some unfortunate mis-understandings regarding the availability, individually or as a whole, of the restaurants of the Haley Group. As I understand you have had face-to-face meetings with various representatives of my firm, I thought it more appropriate to break the bad news and to express my regrets in person. At this time, ladies and gentlemen, the bottom line is that none of the assets of the Haley Group are for sale. I know you have all been led to believe otherwise, and I apologize for that."

She paused to let her words sink in. Almost immediately, the clamor began.

"Not for sale?"

"I've got the paperwork in hand—"

"My investors are already prepared to—"

Grace allowed them to rattle on for a minute before raising her hands. Several more minutes passed until the prospective buyers settled down to silence, or at least to muttering under their breath.

"As I stated," she emphasized, "I am aware that you have all been recently engaged in negotiations to purchase one or more of the Haley properties. And I am very sorry that said negotiations were entered into by one of our board members under false pretenses."

A portly gentleman whose suit buttons were straining to contain a belly that evidenced a great deal of time spent in the dining industry was the first to speak directly to her.

"Madam, it was your very own fiancé who offered me first refusal on the purchase of any and all of your restaurants."

That damn word again.

The rising level of grumbling indicated that he had not been the only one present to receive that same offer.

"Corporate infighting is so irritating, isn't it?" She smiled coldly. "Our publicity department was mistakenly instructed to print that engagement announcement. Mr. Huntington is merely the visible president of the Haley Group, and a minor shareholder at that, who has allowed his personal greed to overstep the bounds of good sense, not to mention the bounds of his authority."

"Are you telling us Charles Huntington is not authorized to sign off on business deals for the Haley Group?" This from a sharply creased woman in unrelieved black. Her pinched expression indicated severe displeasure, not to mention skepticism.

"That is exactly correct. As the owner of fifty percent of the corporation—" she indicated herself "—my approval is necessary for any major business decisions, and I can assure you that I have not approved any of these offers." She smiled gently now and began the process of easing them into acceptance of this sudden about-face. "I understand, of course, that after the merry chase you've been led, you might be inclined to doubt my statements without some further reassurance as to their validity. Which is why I invited our corporate attorney, Mr. Franklin O'Connell, to join us today, so that he can verify what I'm telling you. Franklin?"

The attorney rose from his seat at the table and nodded. She continued.

"It occurs to me that some refreshments might be appropriate while we continue our discussion. Please feel free to speak with Mr. O'Connell while I arrange things. Thank you."

Not until she stepped out of the room into an adjoining office did she allow her shoulders to sag with relief. She was going to pull it off. It was there to be read in their faces already. They believed her, based only on her clear self-assurance, and the questions they would ask Franklin would only reinforce the fact that she was the sole authority in the Haley Group. With exactly fifty percent of the corporation in her name, she couldn't sell off any part of the Haley Group herself, either, but she could certainly block the moves made by Charles and her mother.

She'd just done exactly that.

Picking up the phone, she punched in the number for room service and placed her order, directing them to send the server in with a passkey, so as not to interrupt the meeting with a knock. She stopped for one last glance at herself in the mirror before heading back into the battle zone.

Her hair was perfect. Her hair, her makeup, her Chanel suit and heels, all fit her as if she were born to wear them. And indeed she had been. But she'd unconsciously put her hair up in the same chignon she'd worn to work at Tyler's, and the contrast between her image there and the one that faced her now froze her in place. She felt like two separate women walking around in a single body. One of the women had to be a lie, and she wasn't sure anymore which one she wanted to be true.

Back around the conference table, the conversation was lively but clearly bowing to the inevitable. When the waiter arrived and discreetly arranged a small banquet table along a side wall, nearly everyone accepted a glass of wine or a cocktail. The large gentleman even availed himself of several cold appetizers, the consumption of which had an immediate positive effect on his mood.

"Why don't we remove ourselves to a more casual setting, now that it's clear we won't be doing any business this afternoon?" he suggested with a vague wave toward the casual arrangement of couches and armchairs at the opposite end of the room.

"An excellent idea," Grace answered, and walked with him. The remaining investors followed more or less agreeably. At that moment, she knew without a doubt that she'd won. All that was left were the formalities.

When the glasses were emptied and overcoats and furs retrieved from the closet, when she'd shaken the last hand and bid a firm goodbye to Franklin, she closed the door with a click behind the last well-wisher. A couple of drinks and some charmingly prepared snacks, and they had been uniform in cursing that shameful Mr. Huntington, praising her decision to postpone any further discussion of business for the time being, and begging, every last one of them, to be kept in mind if she decided in the future to reconsider selling.

She'd won. The cold sliver in her heart at how she'd been forced to connive and conspire behind the backs of her onetime boyfriend and her family would go away eventually. Franklin was prepared for her resumption of directorial control as of Monday morning. Grace had taken back her life.

She had less than three days to figure out how to break it all to Tyler.

The golden rays of the setting sun shot through the windows of the Tyler's Bar & Grill and lit up the liqueurs in their glass bottles like rows of jewels reflected in the etched mirror behind them.

To Grace, the slowly dimming light was like a relentless time bomb, ticking out its countdown in a graphic visual display of her eroding time until confession.

She'd managed to avoid intimate conversation with Tyler during the past forty-eight hours, accusing herself of lapsing back into cowardice with every passing minute. As for Tyler, he hadn't questioned her about a thing, including her late and hurried arrival to work on Friday night. He'd simply greeted her with a grin and gruff, "Get to work, or I'm taking a percentage point off your partnership." Even with the joke, she could feel him taking a step back from pressuring her, and wanted to tear her hair out with remorse and frustration. His consideration balanced against her deceit seemed an unfair trade.

But for two days she'd taken guilty pleasure in pretending that all was well between them. She'd smiled until her face ached while she worked in perfect harmony with Tyler at the restaurant, and luxuriated in two nights of falling to sleep, tired but cherished, in his arms. When he'd asked her to run the restaurant for him early Sunday morning so he could take care of some long-delayed personal business, she'd agreed with alacrity, happy to be able to pay back some of the debt she owed him.

The bar phone rang, its attached light blinking as a visual reminder. She delivered a Manhattan to one of her regulars at the bar and snagged the phone on the third ring.

"Tyler's Bar and Grill, this is Grace. How can I help you?"

"Gracie? *Merci.* Thank God it is you."

"Paul?"

The front door swung open and Tyler strolled in, his casual smile instantly brightening at the sight of her behind the bar. He nodded at his customers, dropped a word or patted a back as he passed them, and ducked under the counter to join her. A loud noise dragged her attention back to the phone.

"Paul? I'm sorry. I wasn't listening. What are you so frantic about?"

"Frantic? Frantic? I show you frantic. If I catch that stupid fiancé of yours, with my hands around his neck, I show you frantic. That boy, *idiote,* he—"

Tyler was advancing on her with slow, deliberate steps, and the look in his eye drained her of all ability to think. Her muscles grew weak. She fumbled with the phone as it began to tumble from her hand.

"Paul," she interrupted, "don't worry about Charles. He

can't do anything now. I've taken care of it.'' Her lover's arm curled around her waist and yanked her against his body. "Got to go. Call you soon. 'Bye.''

"But, Gracie, it is necessary to tell you—" His words vanished as she clicked the off button and dropped the phone to the floor.

"Hi.''

"Hi, yourself.''

"How's my bar doing?''

"F-fine,'' she stuttered as his thumb grazed the side of her breast in a slow rise to brush lightly over her lips. Her mind refused to form complete sentences. "Brunch, good. Slow afternoon. Picking up again now.''

"I've missed you all day,'' he whispered before replacing his thumb with his mouth and short-circuiting her entire system. Her body and brain were still reeling as he pulled slowly away from her with a last caress.

"Who's Charles?''

"My ex,'' she answered without thinking, and instantly felt tricked. The words had slipped out before she had a chance to think and she wondered if that had been his purpose.

"Ex-boyfriend, hmm?'' Tyler leaned against the back counter and crossed his arms as he considered her thoughtfully. "He wouldn't be the guy who's been troubling you, would he?''

The thought flashed through her mind that he was entirely too close to the mark. This was followed immediately by the idea that she'd never find a better opportunity to tell him the truth.

"Want me to beat him up for you, Gracie?'' he teased, and tugged at the ends of her loose hair.

"Tyler...''

"What a charming scene, my dear. I do hope I'm not interrupting.''

The oily tones that snaked into her moment of silence from behind her stiffened her back and iced her blood. It was a voice from her nightmares, one whose power she thought she'd taken away. She realized suddenly how wrong she was about that as Tyler looked over her shoulder.

She knew who he saw.

"Can I help you?" Tyler snapped, placing a hand on her shoulder to hold her still, keeping her back to the room.

"I think not," came the upper-crust drawl. "Although you've clearly been helping yourself to my future wife."

She felt Tyler's hand tense and thought he would leap over the bar to defend her. But this was still her battle. Come to confront her in a way she hadn't expected or wanted, but hers nonetheless. She placed her hand on Tyler's chest, looked him in the eye and shook her head.

Then she stepped away from him and turned to face him.

"Charles."

He hadn't changed, his blond hair sweeping carelessly across his forehead, thin lips pursed as if he smelled something rotten, and soft, delicate hands posed artfully in front of him as if he were concerned that if he touched a surface he might catch something. Even his voice, refined in East Coast prep schools and universities and archly superior, was the same.

"Good evening, Grace."

"What are you doing here?"

"Slumming, apparently. The same as you are." His eyes skimmed her clothes doubtfully. "Buying off the rack these days, are we?"

"Stop it, Charles."

"Really, darling—" he waved vaguely at the small restaurant "—this place could fit in the lobby of Nîce. I can't believe you've been hiding out in this shack all this time."

"Shut your mouth." She rapped out the words, her voice raised. Several of the bar patrons shifted on their stools, as if ready to come to her rescue at a word. She saw with pleasure that she'd given Charles a start by yelling at him. He recovered quickly however.

"It seems you've found your temper at last. Charming. I can't imagine that there's anything else worth sampling here."

Her fist slammed onto the bar, rattling the glasses.

"Running an announcement in the papers doesn't make me your wife, Charles, and dining out every night on the company tab doesn't make you a restaurant critic. You don't know anything about value and worth. Just trendiness, and money you didn't have to earn." Dawning nervousness radiated from the matching blue eyes blinking inches from hers. She didn't remember thrusting herself over the bar.

"I repeat, what are you doing here?"

"Well…" He paused, drawing a slim gold case from an inside pocket and carefully extracting a narrow, black cigarette. He looked expectantly at her. When she simply waited, motionless, he exhaled audibly and reached into the same pocket for a gold lighter. He proceeded then to press a button and hold the blue flame to the cigarette tip.

His careful exhale blew smoke directly in her face.

Grace felt the exact moment when Tyler decided he'd had enough. He shrugged off her restraining hand and reached over the bar in a move so fast that the cigarette was out of the other man's mouth and crushed to a stub in an ashtray before anyone blinked.

"I suggest you either answer the lady's question or remove yourself from the premises." He ground the cigarette out even further, leaving a split filter and scattered tobacco. His grin said, *Try me.* "If you can't make up your mind, I'd be real happy to help you."

Grace saw Charles consider lighting another cigarette. He decided against it.

"As I was saying, I've been receiving disturbing information from certain business associates of mine in the last few days." His air of sleazy assurance was less convincing by now. "It seems you've come out of hiding, Grace, and wrecked some of my more carefully laid plans. Once I figured out what was happening, I took Franklin out to dinner and poured brandy in him until he confessed. He always did think you were too big for your britches, darling."

She swore mentally at Franklin. "And I always thought

Franklin was too dumb to be a lawyer. At least one of us was right.''

"That's enough. Before we continue the insult fest, I think introductions are in order." Tyler didn't bother to offer a handshake. "I'm Tyler. This is my restaurant you're standing in."

Her ex smirked.

"Charles Huntington the Third, President of the Haley Group. I'm sure you've stood in more than one of my—of our—restaurants."

But Tyler wasn't even looking at him. His eyes were locked on hers, asking for answers. She hadn't noticed him taking a step away from her, but could feel the distance now. Slowly, he extended a hand toward her.

"I said introductions were in order, Grace." His voice rang sad chords in her heart. "I guess I mean all around."

In her worst, most fearful imaginings, she'd never dreamed it would take place as badly as this.

"Grace Haley."

She shook his hand for what felt like the last time.

"Of the Haley Group." His words were bitter ashes in his mouth.

"Yes."

"How stupid of me." The twist of his mouth cut at her like a knife. "It certainly does shine out of you. I wonder if I would have recognized you eventually." He closed his eyes briefly and she stiffened as he looked at her a moment later. Every trace of her was erased from his eyes. "I don't even want to know what game you were playing here." He laughed, harsh and short. "I always knew you were hiding something. Thought I'd wait until you trusted me enough to tell me. But I never would have guessed this."

"I was going to tell you. Tonight," she whispered as her heart broke and spilled to the floor at his feet. Tyler just looked at her. She could sooner read a stranger's gaze.

"It doesn't matter."

She watched, refusing to believe, as he turned his back on her and walked away. At the far end of the bar, he carefully lifted the counter flap, walked through and replaced it gently. And she was falling, falling into the dark pit that had opened beneath her feet and swallowed her whole. She was sure she must be screaming, but no one seemed to hear her.

What she did hear, from the depths of her fall, as the wind roared in her ears, was Charles's voice, pitched to carry to the corners of the room.

"He didn't know who you were? Or about our engagement, either? My dear, how rude of you. Of course, the staff fall in love with you all the time, and I'm sure you didn't want to make him feel silly, did you?" Charles didn't even try to hide the spite in his words, but it didn't matter. She saw Tyler's step hitch and knew he heard them as truth. "Since Franklin told me you were returning to your old post tomorrow, I merely wanted to drop in to say welcome back, sweetheart."

The slow swing of the kitchen doors marked Tyler's passage out of the room. The noise jarred her enough to shock her back into awareness. Was she letting him leave? This final evidence of her lack of nerve clicked something on inside her. Something she didn't intend to shut off ever again.

She flicked a glance at Charles as she would at a gnat. His self-satisfied grin and fingers that twiddled a goodbye wave toward the kitchen snagged her anger. She scooped up a wet, dirty bar rag and threw it smack in his face.

"You go to hell," she snapped, before racing for the back of the house. "Benny," she shouted without looking back, "show the man out."

"My pleasure, Grace."

The sudden yelp from the bar barely registered as she burst into the kitchen, yelling Tyler's name. She ignored the startled questions of Susannah and Maxie and skidded to a halt in front of the closed office door. She threw it open. He certainly knew who it was.

He didn't look up from his paperwork. The tumble of his hair over his forehead was as familiar to her as her own skin. She'd loved this man, and lied to him. That she'd done it to protect herself was less than nothing. She loved him still, even as she knew she'd lost him. There was only the truth left to try to heal some of the wounds she'd caused.

"You knew I wasn't telling you the truth."

Nothing.

"You knew it. Can't we talk about this?"

At last he looked up. She wished he hadn't when she saw his face.

"Hiding something." He spoke the words slowly, as if testing the shape of them in his mouth. His grimace announced the verdict. "You're right. I knew that. I thought you were hiding from a boyfriend, or had some family trouble."

"In a way, that's—" she began. His voice sliced through hers.

"No, Grace. In no way does my idea of what you were concealing match the truth." His raised hand silenced her protest. "You, one of the heads of this industry, nation-wide, told me that you'd waited tables in a diner once, correct?"

"Yes, but—"

"You are worth millions, and you told me you couldn't afford to rent an apartment, correct?"

"But I couldn't—"

"You're engaged to marry that man, and you told me that you loved me." He dropped his hand as if too tired to hold it up anymore. "Do you remember that, Grace?"

"I was grieving for my grandmother," she said into the waiting silence. "My mother wanted it, and I went along because I was too numb to think. It didn't mean anything, and I broke it off when I left."

In the silence that stretched between them, she could feel him shutting down, forcing his mind and his heart to close off the thought of her. The pain of it struck her like a physical blow.

"I trusted you to tell me the truth when you felt you could." He knew that was true, but the final betrayal hurt too much for that to matter. He looked at her, wondered how she still managed to look so damn fragile to him. "I never thought you'd leave without saying a word."

"I wouldn't do that." The words broke from her with the full force of her love behind them. But even when he knew she told the truth, it sounded like a lie now, to him. "Never. I was going to tell you tonight, before tonight. I just couldn't find a way…"

"To avoid making me feel silly? Do you have any idea how stupid this makes me feel?" Frustration had him punching his fist into the side of the filing cabinet, leaving a sharp dent. The physical pain let him ignore the pain in his heart. "To have offered to share my life, my love, my dreams, with you? Only to find out that you're already worth a hundred times what I will ever build."

"No! That's *not* true," she said, willing him with her eyes to believe her. "You've created something wonderful here, someplace unique and warm, and you know that. So don't tell me I could make you feel small. I've never thought that, and neither have you."

"Grace, you could buy and sell me with your petty cash. But you're right. I never thought that. I did think we loved each other, though, and I thought I had something to offer you." The past tense cut at her already raw emotions, but she didn't flinch. She deserved the words. When he pressed a hand wearily to his forehead, she stood still. She had no right to offer comfort now.

"You did."

"My family loves you, Grace. Yours obviously doesn't. Your work here had value and was appreciated. I don't know if that was true for you before." His pause didn't allow for interruption. "And I loved you." He shook his head. "I'd hoped that would be enough."

"It was." She was crying now, silently, as she spoke measured words. "It is."

"How could it be? How could I offer you anything that would make you want to stay with me?" He stood up and walked around the desk.

"Because I love you."

For a moment he stopped. Stopped and let himself, foolishly, believe for just a moment that she meant it. That this nightmare wasn't happening to them. "Then stay."

She hated saying the words.

"I can't." And just like that, he was lost to her again. "It's important to me and I need to explain it to you. Because if you could know why I lied, you could understand why I have to go back. Please." She placed a hand on his sleeve as he moved to pass her. "I never meant to hurt you. You believed me once when I said that."

"I believe you now. You wouldn't mean to. But you did." He stepped through the door into the kitchen and faced her, expressionless. "Go back to your empire, Grace Haley, where you can treat people carelessly and they'll put up with it for a paycheck. I'm sure that suits you more than we do."

Then he was gone. The light went with him.

After long moments she roused herself enough to look around the small room. It was tiny, crowded with extra supplies and messy with unfilled papers, inventories and receipts. It looked like what it was: the office of a small business growing too large already for its humble beginnings. He'd offered to share it with her, and now that it was too late, now that she could see everything she'd done wrong along the way, Grace realized that she'd never wanted anything so badly in her life.

The sudden, sharp pain in her chest nearly crushed her. She whirled blindly, needing a way out, and crashed into Sarah at the door.

"Grace?" The betrayal in her voice made it all clear.

"You didn't know any of it." Grace shook her head. The laugh that cackled out of her verged on hysteria. "Of course you didn't. He trusted me to tell you. All of you. And now he hates me, because I don't need him to help me."

She stared around her at the three women in the kitchen. Susannah. Maxie. Sarah. She felt accused by their silence. She thought of Addy and Spencer. Of all the people she'd lied to.

"I needed him to love me. And I'm sorry. So sorry."

But there were no apologies for this.

She ran for the back door and stumbled into the alley, leaving everything behind.

Ten

When it became clear that the pain of losing Tyler might actually kill her, Grace threw herself into her work with a single-mindedness that those around her found alarming.

Grace knew better. After all, there was literally nothing else she could do. At home in her condo, she stared at the bare white walls and modern leather-and-glass decor, and wished she were still tucked into a small room under the eaves of Sarah's roof.

One of the first things she'd done upon her return was to send one of her assistant managers to Tyler's restaurant, with instructions to help out in any way necessary.

"Mop the floors if they ask you. I have an obligation to that family," she'd explained briskly to the puzzled woman. "I've left them with a rather large hole in their staff, and I owe it to them to fill it."

The next morning, at 9:25 a.m., her office door was flung open, rattling on its hinges. Tyler had stomped into the room, dragging Grace's employee by a death grip on her wrist. He'd hauled the woman in front of Grace's desk.

"I don't want or need your charity." His palms smacked onto her papers as he'd leaned over her desk and spit the words at her face. She could only look at him, drinking in the sight like a woman dying of thirst. "Trust me. There is no *obligation* to fulfill. My family doesn't need your help."

The iciness of his words had reached her and she'd heard for the first time how she herself must have sounded. Clinical and cold, discharging a debt like the repayment of some paltry social obligation. And knew that for perhaps the first time in her life, she hadn't felt that way, that she truly *cared* about these people.

"Tyler, that is *not* how I meant it." She'd tried to keep her voice level, and cursed her too-close-to-the-surface emotions as it wavered. "I love you, and your family, and I know I hurt you all, in so many ways. This was...the only thing I could think of that might help, at all."

She'd tried not to flinch as he'd thrust a hand in her face.

"Save it, princess. You've done enough already."

The crack of the door slamming behind him had echoed forever in the suddenly silent room, and for the first time in her entire life, Grace had broken into tears in front of an employee.

She'd cut off all contact with Charles and her mother, easy enough to do since he'd taken an extended leave of absence. The memory of their scorn and disapproval contrasted with the vision she still carried in her heart of the family who'd taken her in like a long-lost child, reinforcing her regrets.

And there was a certain pain, too, in knowing that what she'd once held as a secret, that her family did not love her, was now a well-known fact.

She didn't go out. Not only did every restaurant or cocktail lounge or supper club suffer in comparison to the sense of belonging she'd known at Tyler's, she also quickly realized a new truth about the people she'd once thought of as friends. They didn't know her. To be fair, it turned out that she didn't really know them, either. What she'd thought of as friends turned out to be a loose social circle of acquaintances whose class, income and careers made them convenient dinner partners. To her surprise, very few of her friends had even noticed her lengthy absence, and those who had were not terribly interested in the reasons for it. She quietly withdrew herself from their social whirl and knew she would not be much missed.

The nearest approach she made to real friendship was found in the people she worked with. The only time she felt truly comfortable and at home was when she stood on the floor or in the kitchen of one of her restaurants.

So she worked.

She trekked from restaurant to restaurant, spending a large part of her time at Nîce with Paul. During the first two weeks, there were an overwhelming number of problems to deal with, which helped to distract her. If she'd ever doubted her value to the Haley Group, the mess she cleaned up in the days after her return made it clear that she was needed. She had always known that Charles was a figurehead, but even she wouldn't have believed that one person could screw up so badly in a few months.

Grace had personally hired most of the upper and middle managers, however, and after the major issues were sorted out, her very competent staff stepped in and performed with their usual flawless efficiency.

Unfortunately, this left her with very little to do.

She tried to watch television one night, went to the movies another, but she avoided anything that might make her want to laugh or cry. She sat blindly through six violent action flicks, until she lost patience with even that mindless distraction.

In the end, she went back to her restaurants, haunting a different one each night until closing. And it was at Nîce, late on a Saturday night, that what she'd dreaded finally happened. Her first contact with people who had known her only as Grace Desmond, and who undoubtedly knew of her awful betrayal by now.

She'd stopped at the host stand for a moment when the sight

of an elegantly dressed couple caught her eye. The woman looked vaguely familiar, but unplaceable. Not until the man with her turned around and Grace caught a glimpse of the graying, sandy hair pulled back in a ponytail, did she recognize them.

Before she could decide whether to bolt for the kitchen or to stand her ground, Tyler's old boss, who'd threatened to hire her away from him, walked right over to her.

"Ms. Haley."

"Richard." Using his first name seemed too intimate, but she'd never known his last name. The words came awkwardly. "I'm pleased to see you again."

His eyes were kind. "Quite a different life you're leading these days, young lady."

"Not really," she surprised herself by disagreeing, and then realized it was true. "The scale may be different, but the job is basically the same."

"I'm glad to hear you say that. Not everyone would." He hesitated and then continued, "He's very angry."

The tears came instantly, but by now she was an expert at blinking them away.

"It was a terrible thing, what I did."

"I don't know about that." His words were unexpected. "It occurs to me that you had to have some pretty powerful reasons to disrupt your life like that. My glass house isn't built for stone-throwing, and you never struck me as a dishonest person."

Compassion was the last thing she'd thought to receive, and it broke her self-control. Tears fell and her voice was shaky. "Thank you."

"You ought to stop in sometime. You're missed."

Grace shook her head no immediately, wiping her eyes carelessly on her silk sleeve. "I don't think so. He wouldn't want to see me."

"Then maybe you can tell me why he joined my wife and I for dinner tonight."

"Here?" She nearly choked and felt as if her head would twist off as she looked around her frantically.

"Tyler's a man. He doesn't know what he wants. And besides, you shouldn't just let things happen to you, Grace. Sometimes you have to make them happen *because* of you. Think about it." With those final words, Richard squeezed her in a quick hug and caught his wife's attention with a wave. She walked directly over, a familiar shape following two steps behind her.

Surely she made some sort of polite conversation with Richard's wife, but later Grace couldn't remember a word of it. Every ounce of her consciousness froze at the sight of the man who walked toward her.

She recognized the suit he wore. Felt her breath catch because she knew he wouldn't have wanted to appear to dress to impress her. The tie was new. She wanted to know who had bought it for him. He stopped in front of her as any casual acquaintance might do, an expression of polite distance on his face.

She must have said hello.

"Good evening, Grace. It was a lovely meal. My compliments to the chef."

She wondered if it could possibly have cost him as much as it did her, to speak like strangers. She couldn't do it.

"You've spoken to Chef Paul before, actually," she said, hoping the reminder that she'd had help in her deception wouldn't work against her.

He stared blankly for the moment he needed to fish for the memory. She could see the moment he remembered suggesting that she tell her diner work reference to knock off the fake French accent, and for a moment Grace thought he might actually laugh.

But at her hint of a smile, the shutters slammed down.

"Congratulations on your success" was all he said before following his friends out of the restaurant.

She finished out her night somehow, but Richard's final

command lingered in her mind. *Think about it.* And she did.

Late that night in her condo, the Chicago skyline sparkling like a piece of star-strewn sky outside her floor-to-ceiling windows, Grace poured herself a glass of wine, sat on the carpet by the fireplace and thought. Without giving in to her stormy emotions or waves of self-pity, she quietly took stock of her life, and her decisions, past, present and future. What she discovered did not exactly please her.

In recent weeks she'd worn her pride like armor. Pride in her decision to fight her mother and Charles for her company. Pride in her ability to regain control over her life. And she'd been justified. But she'd also assumed that once she'd decided to take charge, she would automatically continue to be strong in all areas in the future.

This, it turned out, was not exactly the case.

Looking at it objectively, Grace realized that she'd sunk almost immediately back into her old patterns of giving up her control, her choices, to outside forces. The better part of autumn had slid by her in a blur of resigned acceptance. The dawning awareness that she would likely always have to jump-start her own empowerment, at least until she managed to carve out some new habits, made her want to weep. And laugh.

She felt exhausted already at the effort required. On the other hand, the possibility of changing her current course thrilled her. To celebrate, she finished the last of the Cabernet Sauvignon as she watched the sun rise over the lake.

Crawling out of bed the next morning after two hours of sleep, she vowed to ignore her raging hangover and start charting that new course at once. She'd done her thinking. Now it was time to act.

She called her attorney.

Three hours later Franklin O'Connell slammed her office door behind him as he left, and Grace smiled. She pressed the intercom button to her assistant with new enthusiasm.

"Please call Elizabeth Han of McDowell, Stein and Han, and set up a meeting at her earliest convenience. Tell her I'd like to offer her the position of corporate counsel to the Haley Group, and I want to arrange it quickly.''

She hadn't talked to Liz in years, but she thought the small, brusque dynamo of an attorney would be pleased to hear from her.

Next, she attacked the corporation's financial balance sheets, looking this time with a clear eye. Days of analysis brought back to her the pleasure of actually using what she'd learned while getting her M.B.A. In the end, she was surprised at the decision she made.

Shaking off doubts like rainwater, she called for another meeting on the Monday before Thanksgiving.

Grace came out from behind her desk to shake hands with the recently hired Elizabeth Han at quarter to ten Monday morning. She'd remembered long hair and baggy clothes, but hadn't been surprised to find Liz in a chin-length hair cut and tailored suits. The stunning Asian beauty and blunt manner were unchanged.

"Are we all set?"

"Good to go. I can handle the paperwork in no time, and if your read on the situation is correct, this ought to be a cakewalk," Liz said, tossing her briefcase in a chair and grabbing a cup of coffee.

"Excellent. They ought to be here any minute."

"Let's get 'em." Liz's grin was almost feral in anticipation.

When Charles walked into her office alone twenty minutes later, flaunting his disregard of the scheduled time, Grace wasn't surprised in the least. She was also certain that he carried her mother's power of attorney in his pocket.

"Let's make this brief, shall we?" she challenged him, already irritated by the sight of his perfectly groomed hair and prissy mannerisms. "I'm taking control of the Haley Group, Charles."

"Are you really?" She wondered if he thought that lazy drawl made him sound important. "Well, your mother will certainly be disappointed that she chose cocktails and gambling in Monaco over fun and games in Chicago, won't she? The last I checked, she and I still control fifty percent of the corporation, so just how do you plan on accomplishing your grandiose scheme?''

"By making you an offer you can't refuse," she said flatly.

For once, her handsome, self-centered colleague looked unsure of himself.

"And if I refuse to sell?''

"Please, feel free, Charles." She smiled coldly. "I'd hoped to split the sale between you two, but I'm sure Mother would be more than willing to pick up a few extra million dollars on her own. After all, you'll both continue to receive your percentage of the profits based on your remaining shares.''

And just like that, it was over.

Thirty minutes and some minor bickering later, the deal was a fait accompli. Grace Haley was president and majority partner of the Haley Group.

Liz packed up her files, promising to have the necessary documents drawn up as soon as humanly possible. "Got big plans for Thanksgiving? You probably feast like a queen with all of these kitchens at your disposal.''

"Not really." Grace laughed. "I try to give them holidays off. No, I'm planning on a quiet day. Maybe a glass of champagne to celebrate our triumph today.''

"You get all the credit for this one, babe. But drink an extra glass of bubbly for me. I'll be fighting off the starving masses. My siblings don't know when to stop having children." Liz waved goodbye on her way out the door, stopping briefly to add, "And don't worry, I'll take care of that other matter we discussed at the same time as all this.''

"Thanks, Liz. Happy holidays.''

That evening, she perched on a stool at a stainless-steel counter in the kitchen at Nîce and regaled Paul with a highly exaggerated version of Charles's bravado and ultimate collapse. In between brow-beating his sous-chefs and line cooks and threatening the servers with bodily harm if they didn't get their orders out of his kitchen in timely fashion, he roared his approval of her strategy and total success.

"*Magnifique, chérie.* And you save his life, too, that fiancé who is no fiancé of yours," Paul announced. "I am getting very close to some bad things with him." He buried his cleaver in a large melon shaped suspiciously like a human head, chopping it in two.

Grace choked on the water she'd sipped.

"Paul!"

He shrugged. "Nobody's fingers go in the pots in my kitchen but mine. There are rules."

She smiled and forked up another bite of Paul's airiest soufflé. Liz's question about the upcoming holiday echoed in her head, and the surge of loneliness she'd hidden at the time inspired her now.

"What are you doing on Thanksgiving, Paul? Why don't you come over to my place?" She added impulsively, "I'll cook a holiday dinner for us."

"Wait." He shifted an enormous vat of simmering soup off a back burner before dipping a large spoon for a taste test. Rolling his eyes and lifting his face to imagined heavens, he paused and then sighed. "*Bon.* Take it." In response to the imperial wave, a busboy lurched under the weight of the pot and staggered off. Paul turned to her. "Grace, I do not think I am ever hungry enough to eat your cooking. Besides, I am preparing the dinner for the orphans."

"The orphans?" she asked, ignoring what felt like a rejection.

"Yes, orphans. These kids, they work here, but some are far from their families. Nine or ten would eat spaghetti at home alone, so I make them the tradition. The turkey, the sweet potatoes, all the trimmings." His eyes nearly sparkled in anticipation. "Three kinds of stuffing. Very good."

She felt the urge to self-pity roll over her like a wave. Stop. Was there anything she could do to change her feelings, or the situation? She found that indeed there was.

"Do you think I could join you?"

* * *

"Hi, Gramma. I'm sorry I haven't come here before now."

The small bouquet of autumn flowers she'd placed at the base of her grandmother's tombstone looked lonely against the cold ground. She'd nearly felt like a part of a large family at Paul's Thanksgiving dinner for the "orphans." The sensation had reminded her that she could in fact visit one member of her family who'd loved her, so she'd directed her driver to this small town north of the city on an impulse this morning. Another area of her life she would take better care of from now on.

"I had dinner with Paul on Thanksgiving. Then I gave him half of Nîce. He cried. You'd have been proud of me."

She brushed the tears away and thrust her cold hands deep into her coat pockets.

"I've done some other things you wouldn't be so proud of. I hurt some people I love very much. One person in particular. I'm not sure I can ever be forgiven for it."

She could practically hear her grandmother's feisty words ringing in her ears. Somehow she laughed through her tears.

"I know. You're right. I'm a Haley." Her voice firmed in the deserted cemetery. "I have a genetic history of ancestors who defined the word tenacious.

"Maybe we're just too stubborn to know when to quit. But as long as there's a chance, I can try to make things happen, my way.

"Wish me luck, Gramma."

Where was her taxi?

Grace paced to the floor-to-ceiling windows that looked out over the front of the building and peered down at the street, as if she could call the cab to her with the sheer force of her impatience, from several hundred feet above street level. She didn't regret giving her driver the night off, but maybe she should've asked if the limo she'd hired to take him and his fiancée out on the town for New Year's Eve could have dropped her off first.

She paced a little more before giving up and striding to her front door. Forget it. She'd wait outside. Maybe she could flag a cab on the street. She stopped a moment at the mirror in her entryway, checking her face and hair for the ninth time in fifteen minutes, and then screwed up her nerve and turned to head downstairs.

Sudden pounding rattled the door on its hinges. She jerked her hand back from the knob like a two-year-old touching a surprisingly hot stove. After two moments of silence, the pounding recommenced, even louder now, if that were possible.

"What did I do?" Grace murmured, and then shook herself out of her startled immobility. Why, in these situations, did she always assume that she'd done something wrong? Feeling guilty as a knee-jerk response was not good. After all, it was very possible that whoever was assaulting her door like a Marine taking Iwo Jima had the wrong condo number.

"Grace!" The thick oak door didn't muffle Tyler's bellow one decibel.

Shoot.

She ought to have guessed. The dratted man had the timing instincts of a birthday honoree who insisted on returning home before all of the surprise party guests had a chance to assemble.

"Grace! Open the damn door."

She shifted her weight from one foot to the other, and then back again. Her velour felt winter hat was rolled into a skinny tube between her twisting fingers. He was ruining everything.

The pounding let up for a moment.

"Go away!" she shouted. "You're ruining it!"

"What? Ruining what? You're the one locked away on the fiftieth floor of some…" His voice trailed away to a low rumbling mutter. The doorknob rattled in its socket. "Damn it, Grace! The doorman hosed me for a hundred bucks and a date with my sister. Open the door."

Her hand was already on the knob, which twisted a little under her palm. She pictured his hand on the opposite end of the mechanism and felt the instant awareness of his physical presence like a blow to the gut. She opened the door.

And took a step back as it flew open and crashed into the wall. Tyler barged through like a man who'd barely resisted the temptation to try to kick the door down. She retreated farther and stepped off the tiled floor of the entry, the heels of her winter boots sinking into plush carpeting. That probably explained her wobbly knees and the fact that her center of balance seemed to have flown out the window.

Yeah, right.

God, he looked good. In a long dark coat, black turtleneck sweater and dark jeans, he stalked toward her like an upscale sailor hitting shore after too many months on a boat without his woman. Make that a pirate. She edged backward and felt distinctly as if she'd just taken her first step down the plank.

"My doorman's going on a date with your sister?" she said, grasping for any conversational straw in the sudden river rush of emotion at the sight of him. "Which one?"

"I don't know your doormen by name, Grace." He was definitely irritated with her.

"No. Which sister?"

"Sarah. She's waiting in the car." He whipped a daily organizer out of his coat pocket and scribbled words on the tiny screen with a stylus as she watched, openmouthed. "Get tinted windows."

"When did you get a Palm?"

"Right after we got reviewed in the *Tribune,* the *Sun-Times* and *Chicago* magazine. All in one week." Tyler shot a sharp look at her from under lowered brows while Grace nodded and tried to look dumb. What were strings for if you couldn't pull one or two? "Not only has business gone through the roof, but I happened to mention that I wanted to showcase local jazz and blues bands someday. Now I'm getting phone calls every day. Bands, people who represent bands, and some guy who wants me to come down to Dallas and open a place there. Crazy. I can't keep track of a damn thing without this computer now."

"Sounds good," she ventured.

"It is. I'm knocking down the wall and expanding into the next building."

"Terrific. Congratulations." She heard herself reduced to babbling as Tyler took a step toward her. "I mean, that was always your plan, right? Expansion. You're just doing it a little…" She dug for the words, came up with nothing and edged farther backward.

"Ahead of time?" When she nodded and gasped, she realized she'd been holding her breath. Her calf knocked painfully into what felt like a coffee table as she shuffled in reverse, trying to keep several steps away from Tyler as he stalked toward her, but unwilling to take her eyes off him. If she didn't know better, she'd swear he was grinning at her, amused by her evasion tactics. "I'm running about two years ahead of schedule, and I know who's responsible for that."

"Tyler, I didn't do anything—"

"I am." He took three quick strides and was on her. She threw a hand up reflexively and smacked her palm against his chest. Keeping him at arm's length was the only thing that might save her from throwing herself at him and looking like a complete fool. Tyler's hands dangled at his sides, but he leaned against her palm, telling her with the weight of his body that he wanted to be closer than this.

She felt the planes of his chest muscles under her fingers. Saw her hand stretch wide open as if to touch even more of him, and knew she couldn't control that movement. Then she realized that Tyler was still speaking.

"I am responsible for it. It was my dream, my vision. I planned it. I built it. And then I hired you. And I was smart enough to take advantage of what you could do for me."

His hands came up and circled her wrists loosely. Her arm was no longer so firmly straight.

"That was pretty smart of you." Somehow she managed to form the words, despite the fact that nearly all her attention was focused on the exquisite sensation of his thumbs moving in small circles on the undersides of her wrists.

"I'm a pretty smart guy." His eyes shone with the light of a thousand stars in a night sky. She felt his steady heartbeat beneath her palm. "Every once in a while, though, it takes me a little longer to catch on.'' His hands tightened on her wrists. ''I love you, Grace, and I want you with me, always. I'll try to adjust to your life, if you'll make yourself a part of mine.''

His face blurred in front of her and she tasted salt in his kiss as she collapsed the space between them in an instant. She clung tightly to him for a moment but then pushed him away, laughing through her tears.

''You idiot!''

She wrapped her arms around his neck and kissed him again, unable to stay away for more than a second. Taking advantage of her living room furniture, she gave him a little push and Tyler toppled willingly to the couch, twisting so that he landed on top of her.

''I thought we'd decided that I was pretty smart.'' He grinned down at her.

''You're ruining my whole plan.'' She pretended to throttle him and then pressed her lips to his neck in apology.

''You had a plan.''

''Yeah,'' she said, looking up at this face she would wake up to every day for the rest of her life, ''and it was a pretty good one.'' Then she knew what she had to do. She moved until Tyler sank beneath her and she lay on his chest. For a moment she considered just staying right here for the rest of the night, but she knew he deserved more than that from her.

She stood next to the couch and beckoned to him.

''Come on. Let's get out of here.''

''Everyone! People! Your attention please!''

Someone cut the music off abruptly.

Like a bug pinned to a mat, was all she could think, as hundreds of eyes focused on her. She was heads and shoulders above the crowd, knees wobbling as she stood on a bar stool in the packed room of Tyler's pub, one hand braced on the shoulder of a stranger at her side.

But only one pair of eyes mattered. She could read the love in them from where she stood. Tyler didn't move, knowing that she needed to do this one last thing to make everything right. Not only between the two of them, but for everyone else she'd met and fallen in love with through him.

Silence fell over the packed room.

"Hi." She didn't know how to begin.

"Hiya, Gracie!"

The familiar face saved her.

"Hi, Benny," she called shakily. At the far end of the bar, Maxie was waving crazily at her, standing next to a smiling Susannah and Addy. Behind the bar, Spencer shut off the Guinness tap that was spilling stout over the top of the pint below it. Sarah had snuck through the crowd and now put an arm around Grace's waist. And with that, the words came. All she had to do was tell the truth.

"Hi, everybody. My name is Grace. Grace Haley. And I'd like to tell you a story." Never taking her eyes off Tyler, she began in the age-old fashion.

"Once upon a time, there was a girl who was in trouble. It was a lot of trouble, but instead of staying to fight her own battles, she ran away. Lucky for her, she ran into a man who liked to take care of strays." That man was looking at her now, and she held on to his gaze like a lifeline with her heart and soul. "A brilliant, wonderful, funny, incredible man, with a terrific family. They took her off the street and made a place for her in their homes. In their hearts. And it wasn't long before she fell in love with them. All of them. But the biggest part of her heart was filled with love for the man."

She could hear the whispers building around her. She ignored them, as she ignored the tear she felt trickling down her face.

"This girl was foolish and not very brave, so she did some stupid things. She lied about who she was and where she was from, because she hoped she could hide from all of her problems. She hadn't figured out yet that you can't hide from the really big ones. That you shouldn't.

"Now, the man was pretty smart, as I said, and he knew she wasn't telling him everything. But he took her in anyways, gave her a job and let her stay, as long as she would promise him one thing. She could keep her secrets, she could be safe with him, he told her. Then he said, *'but on December thirty-first, New Year's Eve, you sign on one hundred percent and there'll be no more hiding for you.'''*

She stopped. Tyler was walking toward her, pushing easily through a crowd that parted for him like mist, never breaking away from her eyes.

She wasn't finished.

"I've made a lot of mistakes since the day you said that, Tyler. But it's December thirty-first, New Year's Eve, and if you still want me, I'm done hiding. I love you, and I couldn't hide that if I tried."

He was at her feet and she was trying to get off the damn stool, but she couldn't see the floor and then she couldn't see anything because she was crying as he kissed her and she was telling him she loved him, over and over again, fiercely, her hands fisted in his shirt as her mouth found his mouth, and his face, and any part of him she could reach. Touching him was coming home and loving him was what she'd been heading toward all her life.

Her face was framed in his hands and she saw her soul in his eyes as he held her. She didn't even need the words when he said them.

"I love you, Grace Haley."

The crowd exploded around them. Richard was ringing the bell as if the gates of heaven had just opened and Spencer was pouring champagne as if the world was ending tonight.

She found herself on the ground at last, surrounded by shouting friends who counted down the last seconds to midnight.

The space between them was a separate world. She threaded her hands through his damp hair and smiled up at him.

"I was coming to find you when you showed up at my door."

"And I always knew I'd find you on the thirty-first, no matter where you'd gone." His smile was soft and his hands moved on her as if he couldn't get enough of touching her.

"Then we were both looking for each other." Which felt right.

"You got it," he answered, and kissed her while confetti rained down on them like drifting snow. When he lifted his head, his smile teased her. "So I've got my waitress back?"

"No way." At his raised eyebrow, she grinned and stood on tiptoe to wrap her arms around his neck. "I've got a much bigger job in mind this time around." She saw him anticipate her words and loved that he knew her so perfectly. "How do you feel about taking on a wife?"

The next moment she found out that he'd beaten her to the idea a long time ago. Reaching into his pants' pocket, he pulled out a small velvet box and held it in front of her.

"I bought this the morning you left."

She curled her fingers over his and leaned in to press her mouth softly to his.

"I'll never leave again."

The clock struck midnight. Horns blared and balloons fell around them. She whispered to her love the words that end all fairy tales.

"And they lived happily ever after."

Tyler spun her around and laughed out loud.

"You bet your ass they did."

* * * * *

Silhouette

Desire

**Coming February 2004
from**

SHERI WHITEFEATHER

Cherokee Stranger
(Silhouette Desire #1563)

James Dalton was the kind of man
a girl couldn't help but want.
The rugged stable manager exuded
sex, secrets...and danger. Local waitress
Emily Chapin had some secrets of her own.
The one thing neither could hide was
their burning need for each other!

***Available at your
favorite retail outlet.***

A sizzling brand-new series by
ROCHELLE ALERS

THE BLACKSTONES OF VIRGINIA

Experience the drama... and the passion!

Three larger-than-life love stories of a powerful American family set in Virginia's legendary horse country.

It begins with:

The Long Hot Summer

(Silhouette Desire #1565)

Don't miss the next thrilling title of the Blackstone trilogy later this year.

Available February 2004 at your favorite retail outlet.

Visit Silhouette at www.eHarlequin.com

SDTBOV

Silhouette®

Desire®

presents

DYNASTIES: THE DANFORTHS

**A family of prominence...
tested by scandal, sustained by passion!**

Man Beneath the Uniform
by
MAUREEN CHILD
(Silhouette Desire #1561)

He was her protector. But navy SEAL
Zachary Sheriday wanted to be more
than just a bodyguard to sexy scientist
Kimberly Danforth. Was this one seduction
Zachary was duty-bound to deny...?

*Available February 2004
at your favorite retail outlet.*

Visit Silhouette at www.eHarlequin.com   SDDYNMBTU

eHARLEQUIN.com

The eHarlequin.com online community is *the* place to share opinions, thoughts and feelings!

- Joining the community is easy, fun and **FREE!**

- Connect with **other romance fans** on our message boards.

- Meet your **favorite authors** without leaving home!

- **Share opinions** on books, movies, celebrities…and *more!*

Here's what our members say:

"I love the friendly and helpful atmosphere filled with support and humor."
—Texanna (eHarlequin.com member)

"Is this the place for me, or what? There is nothing I love more than 'talking' books, especially with fellow readers who are reading the same ones I am."
—Jo Ann (eHarlequin.com member)

Join today by visiting
www.eHarlequin.com!

INTCOMM

The Queen of Sizzle
brings you sheer steamy
reading at its best!

USA TODAY
Bestselling Author

LORI FOSTER

FALLEN ANGELS

Two full-length novels
plus a brand-new novella!

The three women in these
stories are no angels…
and neither are
the men they love!

Available February 2004.

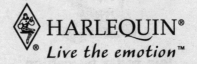

HARLEQUIN®
Live the emotion™

Visit us at www.eHarlequin.com

PHFA

Silhouette®

Desire®

presents

The Long Hot Summer

(#1565)

by

ROCHELLE ALERS

It is the sizzling first title of a brand-new series

THE BLACKSTONES OF VIRGINIA

Ryan Blackstone promised he would never trust a woman again, but sultry Kelly Andrews was just the woman to make him break that vow! But was it love or just lust that irresistibly drew this pair together?

Available February 2004 at your favorite retail outlet.

Visit Silhouette at www.eHarlequin.com   SDTLHS

COMING NEXT MONTH

#1561 MAN BENEATH THE UNIFORM—Maureen Child
Dynasties: The Danforths
When Navy SEAL Zachary Sheriday was assigned to act as a
bodyguard to feisty Kimberly Danforth, he never considered he'd
be so drawn to his charge. Fiercely independent, and sexy, as well,
Kimberly soon had this buttoned-down military hunk completely
undone. But was this seduction one he was duty-bound to deny…?

#1562 THE MARRIAGE ULTIMATUM—Anne Marie Winston
Kristin Gordon had tried everything possible to get the attention of her
heart's desire: Dr. Derek Mahoney. But Derek's past haunted him, and
made him unwilling to act on the desire he felt for Kristin. Until one
steamy kiss set off a hunger that knew no bounds.

#1563 CHEROKEE STRANGER—Sheri WhiteFeather
He was everything a girl could want. James Dalton, rugged stable
manager, exuded sex…and danger. And for all her sweetness, local
waitress Emily Chapin had secrets of her own. One thing was
perilously clear: their burning need for each other!

#1564 BREATHLESS FOR THE BACHELOR—Cindy Gerard
Texas Cattleman's Club: The Stolen Baby
Sassy Carrie Whelan had always been a little in love with Ry Evans.
But as her big brother's best friend, Ry wasn't having it…until Carrie
decided to pursue another man. Suddenly the self-assured cowboy was
acting like a jealous lover and would do *anything* he could to make
Carrie his.

#1565 THE LONG HOT SUMMER—Rochelle Alers
The Blackstones of Virginia
Dormant desires flared the moment single dad Ryan Blackstone
laid eyes on Kelly Andrews. The sultry beauty was his son's teacher,
and Kelly's gentle manner was winning over both father and son. A
passionate affair with Kelly would be totally inappropriate…and
completely inescapable.

#1566 PLAYING BY THE BABY RULES—Michelle Celmer
Jake Carmichael considered himself a conscientious best friend. So
when Marisa Donato said she wanted a baby without the complications
of marriage, he volunteered to be the father. Their agreement was no
strings attached. But once pent-up passions ignited, those reasonable
rules were quickly thrown out the bedroom window!

SDCNM0104